A strange look swept over his face, like a million regrets rushing through him at once.

"Please, Deborah," Cole said. "Let me take you home. It's not safe."

He picked up her bag, his muscles flexing, and she remembered how safe he used to make her feel. Now she felt nothing but regret that she'd allowed him into her life.

She took the bag. "I'll take my chances alone."

"You're letting your emotions override your common sense. You need protection."

He was right. There was a ball of fear in her belly, telling her to be cautious, but she ignored it. Yes, Cole could provide protection, but at what cost to her heart?

"I'll take it from here." She stalked out the door, ignoring her conflicting emotions. Cole's presence could protect her, but every fiber of her body cried out to run from him.

When she reached the parking lot, she heard them.

Footsteps behind her.

She spun around. "Cole, is that you?"

No reply.

"Who's there?"

A menacing voice rumbled, "Your worst nightmare."

Elisabeth Rees was raised in the Welsh town of Hay-on-Wye, where her father was the parish vicar. She attended Cardiff University and gained a degree in politics. After meeting her husband, they moved to the wild, rolling hills of Carmarthenshire, and Elisabeth took up writing. She is now a full-time wife, mother and author. Find out more about Elisabeth at elisabethrees.com.

Books by Elisabeth Rees

Love Inspired Suspense

Navy SEAL Defenders

Lethal Exposure
Foul Play

Caught in the Crosshairs

Visit the Author Profile page at Harlequin.com.

FOUL PLAY

ELISABETH REES

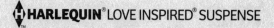
HARLEQUIN® LOVE INSPIRED® SUSPENSE

Recycling programs
for this product may
not exist in your area.

LOVE INSPIRED BOOKS

ISBN-13: 978-0-373-44717-6

Foul Play

www.Harlequin.com

Printed in U.S.A.

He heals the brokenhearted and binds up their wounds.
—Psalms 147:3

For my real life hero, David.

ONE

The life-support machine beeped away in the darkened hospital room, echoing the reassuring sound of a heartbeat through the air.

Senior nurse Deborah Lewis checked the wires and tubes attached to the body of the tiny baby boy. His parents watched closely, grief and bewilderment evident on their faces. The deterioration of their son had come quickly, and they were unprepared.

Deborah put a hand on the mother's shoulder. "He's in good hands here," she said. "Harborcreek Community Hospital has the best pediatric care in Pennsylvania."

One of Deborah's nurse colleagues, Diane White, appeared in the doorway. "Deborah," Diane called into the room. "Do you have a moment?"

Deborah clipped the medical chart onto the end of the steel bed frame and smiled at the couple. "I'll be back soon, okay?"

She joined Diane in the corridor and closed the door. The atmosphere in the pediatric unit was somber. Six children had recently fallen gravely ill; three of them were now on life support. It had been a bleak few days for the medical staff of Harborcreek Hospital, which was just a few miles from the lakeside city of Erie.

Diane held a pile of laundered sheets close to her chest, looking around anxiously as she spoke. "Frank Carlisle has been here," she said in a whisper. "He says he wants to talk to you about something important."

Deborah stood a little closer to Diane, noticing that her friend's baby bump was straining against the fabric of her scrubs. The mention of Frank Carlisle caused a ripple of anxiety to flow through Deborah's body. Frank, the hospital administrator, was responsible for overseeing the smooth running of the entire hospital and was well-known for maintaining a tight ship. News of the sudden spate of emergencies in the pediatric unit had displeased him. Usually she gave Frank Carlisle a wide berth, but in this instance she needed him to listen to her. And to take action. She suspected possible medicine tampering and had raised her concerns with him over a week ago, yet he had done nothing.

"I heard you spoke to him about the number of kids falling sick in the unit," Diane said. "And I also heard you want him to open an investigation. Are you sure that's necessary?"

"I'm really worried," Deborah whispered. "All these sick children are showing signs of renal failure. It just doesn't make sense. Up until now, we've only seen children over ten years old with these symptoms, but now we have a baby with failing kidneys, as well. His body might not cope with the strain."

A hospital orderly passed by, pushing an expectant mother in a wheelchair, and Deborah ushered Diane to one side. "I've never seen anything like it before—six children have been struck down with kidney failure in the space of just three weeks. I'm starting to wonder if someone has been interfering with patient medicine."

Diane clutched the sheets closer to her chest. "Are you serious?"

"Deadly serious," replied Deborah. "Frank thinks I'm being ridiculous, but I told him we need more security in our unit to be on the safe side—cameras, barriers, better alarm systems."

"But there's no evidence of drug tampering," Diane said. "Do you really think Frank will spend that kind of money just as a precaution?"

Deborah raised her eyebrows. "Frank would do anything to avoid a public scandal. The good reputation of this hospital is all he lives for." The pager on the waistband of her pants began to beep. She pulled it off impatiently. "I gotta go to the morgue." She held the pager in her hand, shaking her head. "Why would the morgue be paging *me*?" Then a thought struck her and she gasped. "We haven't had a child die recently, have we?"

"No," Diane replied. "But maybe a dead child has been brought in and taken straight to the morgue. They might need you to do the family liaison."

Deborah sighed. She hoped not, but as a pediatric nurse, that job fell to her from time to time. "Maybe," she said, holding out her hands to take the bedding from Diane's grip. "You want me to take these somewhere for you on my way?"

Diane shook her head. "I'm fine."

Deborah put a hand gently on Diane's growing belly. "Are you sure? If you need a break, please tell me. You're eight months pregnant. You're entitled to rest once in a while."

"I'm okay, honestly," Diane said as Deborah's pager began to beep again. "You go."

Deborah smiled and started to walk quickly down the corridor, feeling her blond curls bounce in rhythm with her sneakered feet. She pressed the button to call the elevator and as soon as she was shut away inside she let the smile fall from her face. Her friend's pregnancy should be a cause for happiness and joy, yet it only served as a reminder that her own biological clock had started to tick. When she had been young and naive, she had assumed she would be a longtime wife and mom by the time she turned thirty, raising a family in the beautiful surroundings of her hometown of Harborcreek, where she lived close to her mom and dad, and a whole bunch of friends who made her feel loved and blessed. The only thing missing from her imagined vision of the future was the man she'd thought she'd marry— Cole Strachan.

She exited the elevator and began walking to the morgue, concentrating on the sound of her rubber soles squeaking on the tiled floor, trying not to remember the day Cole had ended their relationship. He'd done so shortly after enlisting in the navy, telling her that he was too young to settle down, that he needed to live a little. *Come on, Debs,* she muttered to herself. *Ten years is too long to still be grieving. Get over it.*

She fixed her gaze on the end of the long corridor as she walked through the warm sunlight streaming in from the large windows lining the passageway. Cole may have broken her heart but he had not broken her spirit. She was stronger than that.

She walked a little closer to the wall when she saw a man approaching carrying a stepladder. His head was bent over a piece of paper in his hand, no doubt trying to work out his location in this large hospital with its maze of linked corridors. Her pager began to beep again and she yanked it from her waistband, furrowing her brow at the display. The man with the stepladder passed her by, engrossed in studying his scribbled directions, narrowly missing her head with the metal rungs. She considered reprimanding him for his carelessness, but the pager alert had been upgraded to level one. She picked up her pace to seek out the hospital's autopsy attendant, Dr. Kellerman, in order to ask him why a pediatric nurse would be required so urgently in his department.

The morgue was quiet. The front desk where the clerk normally stood to sign in new admissions was empty. Deborah used her hospital security card to open the door of the morgue, feeling the coolness of the room rush over her face.

"Dr. Kellerman," she called. "This is Nurse Deborah Lewis from Pediatrics."

No reply.

"Dr. Kellerman," she repeated, edging her way through the door. "Are you here?"

She walked into the room, averting her eyes from gurneys where deceased patients were covered with white sheets, feet poking from the ends, paper tags tied around gray skin on big toes. She shivered and wrapped her arms around her shoulders, creeping between the rows, heading to the room where the steel refrigeration compartments stored the bodies until collection by a funeral home. A creak on the floor caused her body to give a sharp, involuntary jump. She stopped in her tracks and took a deep breath, shaking her mane of curly hair and mentally chastising herself for allowing the presence of death to cause her this level of unease. She was a nurse. Dealing with loss of life was part of her job. Yet this felt different. This felt uncomfortable, as though the dead were watching her invade their resting place. Her eyes lingered on the stillness of the bodies beneath the sheets. She thought she saw a twitch, a faint hint of a movement underneath a shroud. Her heart picked up pace, and she averted her eyes, telling herself not to be absurd. Her mind was simply playing tricks on her.

Deborah pushed open the dividing door that led into the storage room and called out.

"Hello? Is anybody here?"

The hum of the refrigeration units filled the air in the white, windowless room with steel cabinets covering two walls, floor to ceiling. Each unit had a sturdy handle to slide the compartment out for easy access. One of the units had been left open, cold and empty, ready for its next inhabitant. But there was no sign of Dr. Kellerman or any of the morgue staff.

"Well," she said under her breath. "This was clearly a waste of time."

She turned back to the door that led into the morgue and a gasp of pure terror left her lips. Looming toward her was a shrouded figure, arms outstretched, rasping noises coming from beneath the sheet. Glancing behind the eerie figure, Deborah spotted an empty space on a gurney from where he had risen.

She was stunned into temporary paralysis, watching as the person came ever closer, looming over her, swaying on his feet like a man just learning to walk.

"No," she managed to utter as she felt her body being pushed back. The cold, smooth steel of the refrigeration units slid against her back, and strong, clammy fingers closed around her wrists. Within seconds, she was being pulled toward the open compartment. Her sneakers jarred against the floor as she tried to stop herself slipping, but it was no use. She felt as though she'd been transported into a horror film. This wasn't possible.

Her senses snapped back to full attention, realizing that this scenario truly wasn't possible, and she began clawing, kicking and fighting with all her strength. This was not a dead man rising. This was a living man masquerading as the dead. And he was trying to hurt her.

Her slight body was no match for the large bulk of the man, and she realized with terror that she was powerless to prevent him from pushing her into the refrigeration unit, then holding her down and sliding the box into its place.

She filled her lungs with air and screamed with all the breath in her body as the light faded away. And she was suddenly surrounded by people who would never hear her cries.

Cole Strachan hoisted the stepladder onto his shoulder in the hospital corridor and studied the scribbled directions on the paper in his hand. This place was a nightmare to navigate, and he was hopelessly lost, having walked around for at least half an hour. He balanced the ladder against the wall and decided to take a rest. He knew Deborah worked somewhere in the hospital, but that's just about all he knew. And it was probably all he deserved to know. His belly was a swirl of dread and excitement to think that he might see her again after ten years. Would she have changed? Would she still be beautiful? Would she still have that amazing mane of golden curls? But most important, would she forgive him?

A man in a gray suit turned a corner and came bustling toward him.

"Mr. Strachan from Secure It, I presume?" the man said with an outstretched hand. "I wondered if you might be lost, so I came looking for you."

Cole shook hands and smiled. "You must be Frank Carlisle, the hospital administrator. Am I right?"

The man nodded. "Follow me, Mr. Strachan, and I'll

take you to the pediatric unit so you can have a look around and give us your expert opinion on our security systems."

Cole's heart sank at the mention of pediatrics. The last thing he ever wanted to see again was a sick child. He'd seen enough suffering of innocent children to last a lifetime, and losing his baby son to SIDS two years ago had just about finished him off. That was when he decided to come home to the place he'd been raised. He'd not only left the SEALs in Little Creek, Virginia, he'd left a wife who had divorced him and memories of a son he'd barely had a chance to get to know. Moving back to Harborcreek had been a hard decision, but it felt right. God was leading him back to a place where he belonged. And back to a woman to whom he needed to make amends.

He picked up his ladder and began walking, following the hurried footsteps of Frank Carlisle.

"So you're looking to give the pediatric unit a security overhaul, huh?" Cole asked.

"Indeed we are," Frank replied, leading Cole through a network of corridors. "I chose your firm because I figured that an ex–navy SEAL would give us the best security advice." He stopped and called the elevator. "Your background is very impressive, Mr. Strachan. What brings you to the Erie area?"

"I'm from Harborcreek originally," Cole replied, stepping into the elevator and gently easing the ladder in alongside him. "I recently came home to set up my own security company. It took off straightaway, and I already have ten employees."

"It's nice to have a local man working with us," Frank said. "Most of the staff in Pediatrics are from Erie, but one of our senior nurses is from Harborcreek. Maybe you know her."

Cole's throat seemed to close up and lose its moisture in an instant. "Maybe I do," he managed to say. "What's her name?"

"Deborah Lewis."

The elevator glided to a rolling stop and an army of butterflies began to beat their tiny wings inside Cole's belly. "Is she a petite woman with a lot of blond curls?"

The doors smoothly opened and Frank led Cole into the corridor, using a swipe card to activate the pediatric unit door. "Yes. That's her."

Cole's eyes darted around as they walked into the unit. The walls were brightly painted with cartoon characters, and he caught an aroma of disinfectant and clean laundry.

"I know her," Cole said. "Is she here now?"

"She was supposed to be here for this meeting," Frank said. "But she seems to have gone AWOL, I'm afraid." Frank stopped a female doctor who was walking past. "Dr. Warren, do you know where Deborah is?"

"She got paged," the doctor replied. "To the morgue, I think."

Frank's eyebrows knitted together. "But the morgue staff are on a training day today. They won't be back until 5:00 p.m." He scratched his head. "And why would the morgue page a nurse from Pediatrics?"

Cole detected an edge of concern in the hospital administrator's voice. "How long has she been gone?" he asked the doctor.

Dr. Warren glanced at a clock on the wall. "About an hour or so."

Cole saw the look that passed between the doctor and

Frank, betraying their anxiety. "What's going on?" he asked. "Is there something I should know?"

"Not at all," Frank replied briskly. "I'm sure everything is fine."

Cole narrowed his eyes. "You don't sound so sure, if you don't mind me saying. You sound like you're trying to hide something."

"Frank," Dr. Warren said. "We should go look for her just in case something has happened."

Cole didn't like what he was hearing. "Why would something have happened to her?"

Frank fell silent, so it was Dr. Warren who answered. "Deborah's been asking a lot of questions about sick children in the unit recently," she said, dropping her voice low. "She thinks somebody may be tampering with patient medicine. That's why Frank called you in to upgrade our security."

Frank put his hands on his hips, clearly displeased. "This is all just rumor and suspicion at the moment," he said. "The security upgrade is simply routine maintenance and nothing more."

Cole crossed his arms, letting his instincts lead him where they wanted to go. "Even so, I'd rather go check on Deborah, just to make sure she's okay."

Frank let out a puff of air. "There really is no need, Mr. Strachan. Let's not panic unnecessarily. She'll be back soon enough, I'm sure."

Cole turned without a word and pressed a button to exit the unit. "Okay. I'll go find her myself."

He stepped out into the long corridor that ran alongside the pediatric ward on the fifth floor and pressed the elevator button impatiently. When it failed to arrive immediately, he pushed open the stairwell door and bounded down two at a time. He exited on the first floor, where he remembered seeing a sign for the morgue. He heard Frank's voice behind him. "Mr. Strachan, please wait." Frank caught up with Cole as he slowed to find his bearings. "You can't enter the morgue without an ID card."

Cole stopped and eyeballed the middle-aged hospital administrator, who was looking sternly at him over the frames of his glasses. Cole cocked his head to the side. "Then it looks like you'll have to come with me, after all."

Frank clicked his tongue in exasperation. "Very well." He extended his hand. "This way."

Cole followed Frank's polished shoes, which clipped softly on the floor as he led him yet again through a warren of corridors. As Cole walked, he tried to quell the whirl of emotions stirring deep inside. The thought of stepping inside a morgue was not something that appealed to him. The last time he had been inside a morgue was to collect the body of his precious baby son, Elliot. He had insisted on accompanying the funeral directors while they transported Elliot to their parlor. It was his final job as a doting father. The moment Frank opened the door of the room, Cole recognized the faint but familiar odor of death and he stopped himself from gagging. The memories evoked by smell were often the hardest to bear.

"You see," Frank said, gesturing around. "There's nobody here."

"What about that room?" Cole said, walking to a door at the back.

"That's the refrigeration room," Frank replied. "It's where we store bodies for the longer term. Nobody is in there at the moment."

"I'd like to take a look."

Frank sighed. "If it will put your mind at rest, then please look inside." He walked to the door and turned the handle. "What exactly is the nature of your relationship with Deborah anyway?"

"We were high school sweethearts."

Frank's eyebrows shot up high. "Of course," he exclaimed. "I should've recognized the name. You're *the* Cole Strachan."

Cole was taken aback. Had Deborah spoken of him? "Yes, I'm *the* Cole Strachan. Has she mentioned me?"

Frank gave a wry smile. "A little." He opened the door. "But trust me, you don't want to know."

Cole ignored the comment and walked past Frank into a room with numerous refrigeration compartments. It was empty and quiet, except for a tapping sound coming from behind the wall of steel.

"Someone is trapped in one of these units," he said, feeling his pulse start to race. "It must be Deborah."

He rushed to the compartments and began to slide open each one. Body after body greeted him, pale and lifeless. He and Frank worked together until, at last, Cole saw Deborah slide into view. Her delicate features were unchanged, and her hair was still as lustrous and blond as it ever was. Her eyes were closed, and her body was shaking uncontrollably from the low temperature.

"She may be hypothermic," Cole said, gathering her into his arms, remembering how slender and lithe her limbs were. Her skin felt like ice beneath her thin cotton scrubs.

Her eyes fluttered open. "Cole?" she slurred. "Is that really you? Am I dreaming?"

"Yes, it's me," he said, carrying her through the morgue and out into the corridor, searching for a doctor to assess her condition. "This isn't a dream. I'm right here."

* * *

Deborah sat up in her hospital bed, looking at the anxious faces around the room. Frank Carlisle stood nervously by the door. Dr. Julie Warren was deep in hushed conversation with her colleague Dr. Toby Cortas, and Diane sat close to the bed, holding Deborah's limp hand. Finally, her eyes came to rest on a face she never thought she'd see again in her life—Cole Strachan. He was gazing at her as if the past ten years had never happened. His hair was shorter than he used to wear it, speckled with the tiniest hint of gray among the strawberry blond strands, but his face was still as freckled and youthful as she remembered. His green eyes had always been his most striking feature, and clearly they still were, blinking in his usual languid, unhurried way. He sat leaning forward with his elbows on his knees, hands firmly clasped together as though he were desperately trying to maintain his calm appearance. His clothes were those of a workman: dark T-shirt and blue jeans, tool belt and steel-toed boots. It took her a few moments to realize he was actually here. It had not been a dream or mirage or delusion. Cole was here.

And she wanted him gone.

She fixed him with a stare. "Please leave," she said, before turning her attention to Frank. "I don't want him here."

Diane squeezed her hand. "He saved you from the morgue storage unit," she said gently. "And he hasn't left your side since."

Deborah flicked her eyes to Cole's and lifted her head. He was looking down at the floor. "Thank you," she said tersely. "I guess that makes us even." She heard the hardness in her voice and she didn't like it. This wasn't who she was. "I'm sorry," she said. "I'm grateful you helped me." She let her head flop back on the pillows, still fatigued from the low temperatures she had been subjected to.

Frank stepped toward the bed. "I'm so sorry this happened, Deborah. Dr. Kellerman from the morgue insists that he did not page you. We're looking into it."

"I'll tell you what happened," she said. "Somebody pretended to be dead and then forced me into…" She stopped. The experience clearly had had more of an impact than she'd realized. Cole's presence in the room made her dizziness worse. Her breathing became more labored. Dr. Warren walked to her side and placed a stethoscope on her chest.

"Calm down, Deborah," Dr. Warren soothed. "Slow, deep breaths, okay?"

Deborah could take it no longer. She pointed to Cole and addressed the hospital administrator, who was skirting the edges of the room, hands in pockets. "What exactly is *he* doing here, Frank?"

"Mr. Strachan is here to help us with our security arrangements," Frank replied. "Just like you asked."

Deborah frowned. "So you go and hire a navy SEAL?" she asked incredulously. "Is that really necessary?"

Cole spoke. His voice was an octave lower than it used to be. It was rich and velvety and took her by surprise. "I'm not a SEAL anymore, Dee. I retired six months ago."

Her eyes shot to his and she felt her nostrils flare. His use of her pet name was overstepping, and her glare was intended to let him know exactly where he stood.

Cole produced a business card. "I run a security firm now called Secure It. Frank called me to ask if I could install some extra features to make you all a bit safer." He leaned over and placed the card on her bedside table. She caught a faint trace of his aftershave in the air. "But

I never realized how serious it was until I got here.
Whatever happened to you today was probably a delib-
erate attack, designed to hurt you or scare you, or both.
And I want to get to the bottom of it."

Cole's strong, commanding voice caused the other
four faces in the room to stop and turn in his direction.

"Just hold on a minute," Frank said. "Have you considered that this might simply be a prank gone wrong?
Those guys down at the morgue have a pretty dark sense
of humor, you know."

Dr. Warren exchanged a look of concern with Dr.
Cortas. "Frank," she said. "Another child became sick
today with suspected renal failure—a tiny baby boy.
That makes a total of six in the last three weeks. Deborah
was the one who initially raised the alarm, and she's the
one who's been pushing for an investigation, as well as
extra security on the unit. That certainly would mark her
as a target for anyone tampering with patient medicine."

Frank closed his eyes and put a hand on his forehead.
"The toxicology reports have all come back clean on
these patients." He opened his eyes. "There is simply
no evidence to suggest foul play."

Cole stood up. Deborah had forgotten how tall he was.
His full height dwarfed everyone around him. "Deborah was attacked," he said. "That's evidence enough
for me that she's onto something, and somebody wants
to stop her."

"Let's wait until an investigation is complete before
we jump to conclusions about an attack," Frank said.
"The morgue staff are being interviewed by hospital
security guards, and CCTV footage is being analyzed."

Cole let out a snort of derision. "I met your security
guards on my way in here. I very much doubt they could
find a GI Joe in a toy store."

Deborah suddenly felt a tear spring entirely un-prompted from her eye and land on her cheek. She tried to brush it away quickly, but Diane saw it and turned to the men in the room. "You're upsetting Deborah. She doesn't need this now. She needs time to recover."

Cole swiveled to look at Deborah. She refused to meet his eye, but in her peripheral vision she saw him rub his fingers roughly over his face, coming to rest on the cleft in his chin. She bowed her head low. Her tears were coming too fast to stop them, and he was the very last person she wanted to see her raw emotions.

"I'm sorry, Deborah," Cole said. "It's insensitive of me to argue while you need to rest." He gesticulated toward the door. "Shall we all leave Deborah in peace for a while?"

"Thank you," she whispered, watching the staff members leave the room until just Cole remained standing by the door. He opened his mouth to speak but seemed to change his mind. Instead, he looked at her, apparently waiting for her to acknowledge him, and she raised her head, meeting his gaze with steeliness, wiping the wetness from her cheeks.

"Close the door behind you," she said flatly.

His face was pained as he gave a small nod. After the door clicked into place and she was alone with her thoughts, she picked up the small white card Cole had left on the bedside table. She rubbed her fingers over the gold embossed letters of his name, before taking the card gently between her thumb and forefinger and tearing it into teeny, tiny pieces.

Cole stood opposite Frank in the corridor with a cold and heavy sensation weighing on his chest. The iciness with which Deborah had looked at him was hard to bear.

This woman who had once run through a thunderstorm to tell him how much she loved him now felt nothing but bitterness and regret. And who could blame her? He had broken all his promises. He had abandoned her without warning. But he sure wasn't going to abandon her again, not when she so clearly needed somebody to protect her. This was the least he could do for her.

"I'd like to start work right away," Cole said to Frank. "I'll do a thorough check of all your current security arrangements and compile a list of changes I advise you to make."

Frank shifted uncomfortably. "What kind of price are we talking about here?"

Cole raised his eyebrows. "What kind of price do you put on the safety of your patients and medical staff, Mr. Carlisle?"

"I would like to stress that these measures are just routine," Frank said. "Despite the recent uptick in renal problems, we have no proof of drug tampering. It's likely a coincidence."

As if to mock the hollowness of his words, the hurried figure of Dr. Warren rounded a corner and pushed past them. "One of the kids has gone into acute renal failure. We need to get him on permanent dialysis before his organs totally shut down."

"No," Cole said under his breath, watching the staff rush into a room with a machine that they quickly connected to the body of a young boy, already yellow and jaundiced from the toxins in his blood.

Cole bowed his head and prayed for the life of this child, remembering the lives of many children he had already seen lost on the fateful Dark Skies mission in Afghanistan four years ago. He remembered the life of his own son, taken too soon to reside with his Heavenly

Father. God had certainly never shielded Cole from the painful reality that children die, and He clearly wasn't about to start now.

Cole silently acknowledged that something sinister had brought him back to Harborcreek and back to Deborah. Like the children in this unit, Deborah was in trouble, and whether she liked it or not, he would stick by her side and see her safely through. He couldn't offer her all the things he had once promised, and she wouldn't want them from him now anyway. But maybe if he could look after her for a little while, he would be able to somehow atone for the wrong he had done.

TWO

Deborah sat on the edge of the bed as Dr. Cortas gave her one final health check before allowing her to go home. She felt odd being in a sweat suit when she should have been in scrubs. She had stayed in the hospital overnight, being monitored for the potentially damaging aftereffects of her hypothermic state, and Diane had kindly gone to her home to pack an overnight bag.

Deborah's night of sleep had been broken, full of nightmares of a shrouded man looming toward her. In her dreams she had managed to pull the shroud from the man, revealing his face as Cole's, and she'd awoken with a start, dread invading her bones. Where was the true fear in her situation? Was it the man in the morgue, or was it Cole? Both men had strong power over her emotions.

She could scarcely believe Cole was here, looking as lean and handsome as the day he had promised to marry her. She knew they had been young at the time—only nineteen years old—but it had seemed so natural. They wrote constant emails to each other after he enlisted in the navy, but Cole's correspondence gradually tailed off as he talked more and more about the new and exciting life he was leading. Shortly after his twentieth birthday, he had paid her one final visit, giving her the news that their relationship was over. That was the last time she had seen his face, although she continued to hear of his progress in the military through the grapevine in Harborcreek. He successfully made it all the way to the navy SEALs. And she also heard that he had gotten married. That particular piece of information had pierced her heart like a shard of shrapnel.

"You're fortunate, Deborah," said Dr. Cortas. "Any longer in that refrigeration unit and your hypothermia would have been severe," He held her head in his hands to focus on her pupils. Dr. Cortas was a fairly new doctor to Haborcreek Hospital and revealed little of himself to others, but he was an exceptionally gifted physician, and Deborah felt reassured by his assessment. "You appear to have recovered well," he continued, writing on her medical chart. "You can go home. Frank has put you on sick leave for the next three days."

As if he had heard his name being mentioned, a soft knock echoed on the door and Frank's head popped into view. "How do you feel, Deborah?" He opened the door wide and Cole's large figure came into view. He was standing in the corridor wearing a snug-fitting black T-shirt and blue jeans.

"I've discharged Nurse Lewis," Dr. Cortas said with a smile. "She's doing fine."

"Excellent news," Frank said, stepping into the room. Cole followed. "I want you to take some time to recover, Deborah. Don't even think about coming back to work until you're ready."

Deborah couldn't stop her eyes from flicking down to Cole's wedding band finger—it was bare. He noticed her glance and splayed his fingers out wide, telling her what she wanted to know. She was annoyed with herself for being so obvious. She didn't want him to read too much into it.

"What did your internal investigation uncover?" she asked Frank. "Did you find the man who assaulted me?"

"Not exactly," he said.

Cole narrowed his eyes at Frank. He clearly wasn't happy with this response. "There was a camera positioned right over the morgue entrance," he said. "What did you find on the footage?"

Frank looked sheepish. "The camera isn't working, I'm afraid. It would seem like a good idea to extend our security upgrades to the whole hospital. Can you cope with that Mr. Strachan?"

"Absolutely. I'll get my entire team on it," Cole replied. "But we still need to find out who attacked Deborah. Did you uncover anything? And did you call the police?"

"I decided not to involve the police at this stage," Frank said. "Dr. Kellerman concurs with me that this could be a childish prank gone wrong. The morgue staff have been known to try to scare each other by hiding under sheets." He threw up his hands in the air. "Of course, none of them will admit to being the culprit."

"No!" Deborah said firmly. "Pranks are meant to be funny. What happened to me was terrifying."

Cole stepped back into the conversation. "And why would the prankster leave Deborah locked in a compartment? She could've died."

Frank obviously had anticipated this question. "The compartments have an unlocking mechanism on the inside. It should be fairly simple to slide open the unit from inside by pushing on the door, but this particular one had faulty springs, so it was jammed."

"That could be why the attacker chose this exact unit," said Cole. "He knew she'd be trapped."

Frank looked exasperated. "It's highly likely that this is a prank gone terribly wrong. The hospital deeply regrets it, and it will never happen again. Trust me."

Cole folded his arms. "That doesn't satisfy me at all, I'm afraid. What precautions are you taking to ensure Deborah's personal safety?"

"We're implementing all the recommendations you made regarding our security," Frank said. "At considerable cost to the hospital, I might add. All our workers are perfectly safe here."

"What about when Deborah is at home?" Cole said. "How safe is she there?"

Frank smiled in a condescending way. "I'm certain that you're overreacting, Mr. Strachan. I expect your military training encourages you to see danger all around, but here in Harborcreek, we don't need to be on constant guard."

"What about the children in renal failure, Frank?" Deborah challenged. "Do they need to be constantly guarded? Can you be sure that somebody isn't tampering with their medicine?"

"Deborah," Frank said, putting his hand on her shoulder. "This is a hospital. It's not unusual to have a large number of sick children suffering kidney complaints." He looked toward the doctor. "Isn't that right, Dr. Cortas?"

Dr. Cortas clicked the top of his pen and slid it into his breast pocket. "It's not beyond the realm of possibility," he said. "But it is highly unusual."

Deborah noticed the doctor's dark eyes dart around the room before he excused himself and left.

"I understand your concerns, Deborah," Frank said. He sat on the bed beside her. "And by the time Mr. Strachan's team has finished upgrading our security measures, there will be no way a staff member could harm them—even if that were happening."

Deborah stood up. "Frank," she said, bending to look him in the eye. His eyes were slightly bloodshot, as though his sleep had been as broken as hers. "If there is even the slightest doubt that drugs have been tampered with, we should involve the police."

The mention of police caused Frank to stand bolt upright. "And what exactly should we say to the police? Should we tell them that we have lots of sick children in a hospital?" He let out a sigh. "We don't know that the incident in the morgue is in any way related to the renal failures. You can't ask the police to investigate a hunch."

Cole stepped between Frank and Deborah. "It's not just Deborah's hunch. Both Dr. Warren and Dr. Cortas also seem concerned about the high level of renal failure in Pediatrics."

Frank rubbed the back of his neck. "Do you have any idea what a police investigation could do to the reputation of our hospital? It could destroy the good name we've worked hard to build up. I'm sorry, but I won't allow it unless it's absolutely necessary." With that he turned and stalked out the door.

Cole shook his head and turned to Deborah. "I guess that's the end of that conversation. You ready to go?"

She took a step back from him. "Are you offering to take me home?"

"Sure. I got a team of support guys doing the work here, so I'm free to give you a ride."

She looked up into his face. His stubble was the color of a burned sunset. "No, thanks. I'd rather make my own way."

His jaw clenched. "Please, Deborah, let me help. It's on my way home anyway."

"*You* live in Harborcreek?" she exclaimed.

"I moved back three months ago."

Deborah found her mouth opening and closing, unable to form any words.

"I've kept to myself," he said quietly. "I didn't want to risk running into you before you had the chance to find out I was back."

"So when were you going to tell me?" she challenged. "In another ten years?"

"I'd planned to call your parents this weekend and ask them to tell you I was back in town. I kept putting it off because I was worried how you'd take the news."

Only one word formed in her mind. "Coward."

He nodded his head. "I deserved that. You're right. I handled it badly. I just didn't want to hurt you any more than I have already."

"Why did you come back anyway?" Her question sounded like an accusation.

Cole pushed his hands deep into his jeans pockets. "It's a long story."

"Did your wife move here with you?" she asked.

He closed his eyes. "No, she divorced me a couple of years back."

Deborah stood in silence for a few moments. Despite her hostility toward Cole, she didn't revel in the breakdown of his marriage. "I'm sorry to hear that," she said.

"What about you?" he asked. "I see you don't wear a ring, either."

"I'm not married," she said. "I was engaged to somebody for a while, but it didn't work out."

A strange look swept over his face. It was one of both surprise and disappointment, as if a million regrets rushed through him at once. "Please, Deborah," Cole said. "Let me drive you home. It's cold and rainy out there."

He picked up her bag from the bed, his muscles

flexing beneath his T-shirt, and she remembered how safe his physical strength always used to make her feel. Now she felt nothing but anger and regret that she had ever allowed him into her life.

She reached for the bag and wrested it from him. "I'll take my chances alone. The bus is always busy, and nobody would try to attack me in public."

"You don't drive?" he asked, obviously remembering the fact he had given her a few lessons in his car before they broke up.

"No, I don't drive," she said. "I manage perfectly well without a car. I make this bus journey every day, so you really don't need to worry."

Cole looked skyward as if trying to keep his cool. "You're letting your emotions override your common sense. You need protection. Don't cut off your nose to spite your face."

She knew he was right. A ball of fear was curled up in her belly, telling her to be cautious, to be on her guard, but she ignored it. Yes, Cole could provide protection, but at what cost to her sanity?

"Thanks for all you've done to help me," she said. "But I'll take it from here." With that she stalked out the door and headed for the exit. He didn't try to follow her, but she knew he was watching her leave, no doubt shaking his head at her stubbornness. She put aside the voice in her head telling her to stop, to turn around and take him up on his offer. Instead, she called the elevator and pressed the button to take her to the basement floor, where a bus stop was situated in the underground parking lot for the hospital staff. As the elevator glided below ground, Deborah clenched her teeth together, gripping her bag with tight fingers, trying with all her might to contain her rising level of conflicting emotions.

On the one hand, Cole's presence gave her a sense of reassurance that he could shield her from another attack, but every fiber of her body cried out to run away from him.

She carried her head high as the doors opened and she strode purposefully out into the parking lot, keeping her wits about her, checking her surroundings. The lot was full of cars and empty of people, as it usually was at this time, and the bus stop was near to the exit ramp just around the corner. It would take her only two or three minutes to walk there.

She heard the squeal of rubber tires turning quickly on asphalt and she darted between two cars, crouching low to see where the vehicle was located. A beat-up red compact came into view, radio blaring, a young man at the wheel chewing gum. He raced past her driving way too fast and was soon out of sight. She stood up, exhaling in annoyance as she heard his car scrape its underside on the exit ramp. He was a young hospital orderly, immature and reckless.

But the sound and sight of normal everyday activity reassured her, and she weaved between the vehicles, resuming her walk to the bus stop, where she reckoned several other people already would be waiting. That was when she heard footsteps behind her keeping pace with hers. They were heavy, those of a man, and she suspected that Cole had followed her to try to persuade her not to travel home alone.

She spun around. "Cole…" She stopped. The sound of footsteps melted away, and a hush descended over the lot. Nobody was there.

"Cole?" she repeated. "Is that you?"

No reply.

"Who's there?" she called.

A menacing voice rumbled in the windowless lot lit by dim overhead bulbs. "Your worst nightmare."

Panic hit her full force in the gut, and she dropped her bag and started to run. The heavy footsteps resumed behind her, and she cried out, trying to alert the people who would be waiting at the bus stop just around the corner.

"Help!" Her voice was weak with fear and she filled her lungs to shout louder.

Before she could make another sound she became aware of a person close behind, seeming to appear from thin air. A hand curled over her mouth, another around her throat. They were large hands, rough and calloused, exactly like the ones on the attacker in the morgue. Her screams were stifled, and her legs gave way.

Cole had been right. She had been foolish to refuse his offer of protection. And now she would pay a heavy price.

Cole turned the wheel of his cargo van sharply in the hospital's underground parking lot, sending unsecured equipment in the back crashing to the floor. He saw Deborah, fighting hard with a heavyset man who had grabbed her by the throat. Despite being petite in size, she was holding her own, using her elbow to repeatedly strike the man in the ribs.

Cole screeched his vehicle to a halt alongside the pair, and the man released his grip in surprise. The scarf that the attacker had tied around his face left only his eyes visible, and Cole saw them widen in shock. The guy turned on his heel and ran. Cole jumped from the driver's seat and darted toward the assailant. The man pulled a handgun from his pocket as he glanced back, and Cole decided pursuit wasn't worth it. A hospital was no place to begin a gun battle. Plus, there was someone who needed him to stay right there. He watched the man run to the exit door and push it roughly open. He was headed for the street, not the hospital. At least that put his mind at rest.

He rushed to Deborah's side. She had sunk to her knees and was gasping for air. He gathered her into his arms and pulled her to her feet, waiting for her to catch her breath. Then he lifted her onto the passenger seat of his van and reached for a bottle of water in the cup holder.

"Here," he said. "Drink this."

She sipped the cool liquid slowly, coughing occasionally and rubbing her neck where pressure had been applied.

"The guy's gone," he said gently. "We should go back inside and report this."

She shook her mane of blond curls. "I just want to go home," she replied. "I'll make the calls from there." She continued to rub her neck. "I don't want to stay here one second longer."

Cole put a hand to her cheek. "Did he hurt you?"

Deborah set her amber eyes on him. "Just my pride," she said. Her pale heart-shaped face was partially hidden by the mass of curls that used to fall against his face whenever they kissed. "You were right, Cole. I did need protection. I just didn't want it from you."

"Yeah, I guessed that," he said, removing his hand from her face and placing it on his holstered weapon instead. "That's why I decided to take matters into my own hands. I was following you. I couldn't rest knowing you could be attacked again."

She gave a half smile. "I always used to hate it when you were right."

He laughed. "I remember."

She screwed the top back on the water bottle. "Will you take me home, please?"

"Sure."

He made sure she was safely belted in and then cast an eye across the lot before settling himself in the driver's seat. Slowly, he drove from the basement of the hospital and out into the dull, gray September day.

He glanced over at Deborah. "You'll need to show me the way. I don't know where you live."

"Head for the high school," she said. "It's not far from there."

Her voice was small and she had pressed her body against the door, holding on to the handle as if her life depended on it.

"You're okay now, Debs," he said reassuringly. "I'm here."

"Why is this happening?" she asked. Her question wasn't directed at him—it was directed at a higher being.

"Something bad is going on in the pediatric unit," he said. "And you're trying to expose it. That makes you a target for somebody."

She turned her body to face him. "But who would hurt a child?"

"I don't know." He swallowed hard as memories of the navy SEAL Dark Skies mission forced their way into his mind. "But trust me. There are some people who don't have any morals when it comes to hurting children."

"Do you…" she began. "Do you have any children?"

"I did," he said quietly. "I had a son. His name was Elliot." He took a deep breath. "He died at three months old." Cole didn't look at Deborah's face, but he sensed her horror. "It was sudden infant death," he explained. "Nobody's fault."

"Oh, Cole," she said, her voice thick with emotion. "I'm so sorry."

"My wife petitioned for divorce shortly afterward. She said we should never have gotten married in the first place." He felt awkward, uncertain whether Deborah wanted to hear the intimate details of his life. "I was prepared to work at it, but she wanted out. And she was probably right. We were never suited."

"So why did you marry her?" she asked, her attention suddenly fully on him.

"I don't want to be talking about me, Debs," he replied. "We should be talking about you and the situation at the hospital."

"I need some time to process everything that's happened," she said. "It would take my mind off things if we kept the focus on you. Just for a little while."

"Okay." He understood the need to delay facing an unpleasant truth, and he was willing to oblige. "I wanted to settle down," he explained. "I wanted a happy family. I didn't stop to think that the person to share it with was more important than the romantic picture in my head. Kids should be a bonus to a happy marriage, not the glue that binds it together." He shrugged. "But I won't make that mistake again. It's the single life for me from now on."

"You don't want to be a dad again?" she asked. "But you always said you wanted a whole football team."

Cole thought of his last overseas mission in Afghanistan. He thought of the systematic and deliberate destruction of girls' schools by terrorists, and of the bodies he had been forced to bury.

"A lot can change in ten years," he said solemnly. "An awful lot. I'm not the same person I was."

Harborcreek High School came into view as he drove

through the town. They both watched the large, sandy brick building fade into the distance in the mirror, lost in their own memories of happier times. It only highlighted the gulf that had grown between them.

Deborah pointed to a street off the highway. "Turn here."

She guided him through a neighborhood of new homes. Over the years Cole had often wondered where Deborah lived—was it the type of house she had always wanted? As he pulled up outside a small cottage-style home, he saw that it was. It had a neat front yard and a porch with lavender wound through the frame. The red shutters around the windows shone brightly against the pristine white wooden exterior.

"I'll check the house over," he said, turning off the engine. "And then you need to report this latest incident. Your hospital administrator should contact the police and put some special security measures in place for you." He turned to face her. "But until that's done, I'm not leaving your side, okay?"

Deborah's expression was hard to read. "You're not responsible for my safety, Cole," she said. "You're a busy man with a job to do."

"Everything else can wait." He opened the door. "At least let me come in and scout the place out before we talk about it."

She was clearly trying very hard to affect an expression of strength and calm, but he easily saw the flash of fear in her eyes. "Thank you, Cole. I'd appreciate that."

He smiled. Deborah was still as beautiful as the first day he had asked her out, yet the shine in her eyes had become dull, and she looked tired. He was angered by the thought that a man was determined to hurt someone as kind as Deborah. He stepped from his cargo van and slid his gun from its holster.

Apprehending that cowardly man was now at the top of Cole's agenda, and he would not waver until the threat was neutralized.

Deborah unlocked her front door as a sensation of sickness rose in her throat. She had loved her home ever since purchasing it five years ago and hated that dread had replaced her feelings of security. The man who had attacked her in the morgue and the parking lot had left an imprint of fear on her mind that she just couldn't shift.

Cole opened the door slowly and held his gun close. He put a finger to his lips and indicated for Deborah to stay close to the open door. He opened her kitchen cabinets, checked under the couch, behind drapes, even in her trash can. She leaned against the wall, watching him walk slowly upstairs, his face stony and expressionless. She heard him walking through the two bedrooms upstairs, hating the fact that she was reliant on him for peace of mind. He was the last person she wanted to rely on ever again.

He returned with a smile on his face. "All clear." He holstered his gun. "Why don't you make the call to the hospital while I fix us some tea."

He walked into the kitchen and began opening cupboards as though he were a regular visitor. She bristled at the intrusion, yet she swallowed the irritation and said nothing. She picked up the phone and punched in the hospital administrator's direct number.

Frank answered with his usual curt greeting. "Frank Carlisle."

While she explained the incident in the parking lot, Cole mixed up some iced tea in a jug, occasionally glancing over at her with an expression of support and concern. His effect on her was still strong, causing her stomach to leap and flip, and she turned around, putting him out of her sight. How was it possible that he could still cause such a physical reaction after all these years?

"Well, this is a terrible thing to happen to you, Deborah, especially after the incident in the morgue." Frank sounded genuinely shocked. "I'll report it to the police right away. We'll need to issue a warning to all hospital staff that we have a mugger on the prowl."

Deborah squeezed her eyes tightly shut. "This wasn't a mugging, Frank. The guy was trying to hurt me. He had his hands around my throat."

"Are you okay?" Frank asked. "Why didn't you come back inside the hospital immediately? You shouldn't have gone home alone."

"I'm not alone," she said, dropping her voice. "Cole Strachan is with me. He brought me home after chasing off the attacker."

After a moment's silence, Frank said, "I see. Well, that's a good thing. An ex–navy SEAL makes a perfect bodyguard."

"Don't you see, Frank," she said, feeling that he was making light of her ordeal. "This second attack proves that I'm being targeted for a reason, most likely because I'm close to uncovering drug tampering at the hospital."

Frank let out a long, weary sigh. "These two incidents may be entirely unconnected. I can't help but feel that you're beginning to sound a little paranoid."

"Paranoid!" she repeated incredulously. "You weren't the one shoved inside a freezer compartment or choked by a masked attacker. I am not paranoid."

"Okay, okay," Frank said calmly. "I'll file a report with the police, and we'll let them decide whether there is a correlation between the two incidents. Take some time to rest and recover. You sound exhausted."

She turned around and saw Cole sitting at her kitchen table. "I am," she admitted. "I got the wind knocked right out of my sails."

"I apologize, Deborah," Frank said in a sudden rush. "An emergency call is coming through. I have to go. Take care."

The line went dead, and Deborah went to join Cole at the table, sitting opposite and running her finger down the icy condensation on her glass of iced tea.

"Frank thinks it was a mugger," she said. "He still doesn't believe me about the drug tampering."

"Yeah, I kind of figured that from your side of the conversation."

He pulled his chair closer to hers. "I can help you," he said. "I saw that you have a guest room upstairs—"

She cut him off. "No!"

"I'm trained in special ops, Deborah," he said. "If anyone tries to get to you here, I can be ready—"

She cut him off again. "I said no."

He shook his head. "You always were stubborn."

She met his gaze. "And you always were persistent."

"I prefer the word *determined*," he said, raising an eyebrow, clearly trying to make her smile. It didn't work.

"I can't let you stay here, Cole, not even for one night." She dropped her eyes. "I find it really hard to be around you. I wish you'd warned me you were coming back. I feel like you blindsided me."

"I'm sorry, Debs," he said. "I just didn't know how to tell you."

"I know it's been ten years, but the hurt is still there." She thought of the sunny day they both had sat in a coffeehouse by the lake. His words *too young to settle down* had hit her like a blow to the stomach. "I need time to accept that you're back in town," she said. "It's a lot to take in."

"Okay," he said, leaning back in his chair, putting a larger gap between them. "I totally understand. But you really shouldn't stay here alone. Is there somebody you can call?"

She swallowed away the lump in her throat. "I'll call my brother."

"You promise?"

"I promise." She rubbed her temples where a dull throb had begun. "I know Chad's off work today, so he'll be able to come over right away. You can go."

"I'll stay until Chad arrives."

Deborah's head started to pound. "No," she said. "I need some space." She tried to level her voice and iron out the wobble. Cole's proximity to her was overwhelming. "You're crowding me a little."

Cole reached into his back pocket and pulled out a card. It was the same business card he'd handed to her the previous day. He laid it flat on the table. "My numbers are here," he said. "Call anytime you need me. And I mean anytime."

She picked up the card. "You gave me one of these already."

His mouth curled at the corners. "I'm kinda guessing that it might have ended up in the trash."

Her color rose. He still knew her well.

"I live over on Franklin Street," he said. "So I can be here in just a few minutes. I keep my cell with me at all times."

She nodded. He rose from his chair and headed for the door. His shoulders were much wider and firmer than they used to be. He looked like a man now, rather than the boy she used to know.

"I'll come by tomorrow on my way to the hospital," he said. "Make sure you keep the doors and windows locked tight, okay? If Chad can't come straight over, call me immediately."

She nodded again. He slipped through the door and shut it behind him. She took a deep, steadying breath and sipped her iced tea before dialing her brother's number.

Chad was more animated than usual upon hearing Deborah's voice. "I heard some news today," he said, interrupting her greeting. "Cole Strachan has moved back to town. A friend of mine saw him at the hospital today. I wondered if you saw him, too."

"Yeah," Deborah replied flatly. "I saw him."

"Are you okay, sis?" Chad asked, trying hard to be sympathetic. "Do you want to talk about it?"

Deborah sighed. "No, I don't want to talk about it."

"Are you sure? You sound really down."

"Actually," she said, "I had a scare at work today, and I wondered if you could come over, maybe stay the night?"

"What happened?" Chad sounded concerned.

How could she explain the situation without worrying him even further? "I'll tell you about it when you get here."

"I got called into the office on short notice," Chad replied. "We're working on a big presentation. I'm here till late. Sorry, sis. Is this serious? Can you call somebody else?" Without waiting for her reply, he continued, "Is this something to do with Cole? Did he upset you today? Because if he upset you, I'll make sure he never bothers you again."

"No, Chad," she said. "Can we stop talking about Cole, please?"

"Sure we can. Sorry. Listen, I'd love to come over any other time, but I can't tonight. Call one of your friends or Mom. Don't be alone, okay?"

"Okay, Chad. Don't work too hard."

He laughed. "I never do."

After hanging up, she started to punch in her parents' number. Her mom or dad would surely be able to stay with her tonight. Then she thought of all their questions, their interest in Cole, their desire to defend her against her ex-finance's intrusion back into her life. She simply didn't know if she had the emotional energy to cope with Cole Strachan being the number one topic of conversation. She placed the phone on its base and stood in her living room, contemplating her options. Her house was pretty secure, with strong locks on all points of entry. She would be safe here alone for one night. She could make a plan tomorrow after a good night's rest.

She pushed down the feeling of guilt at breaking her word to Cole. After all, he had broken the biggest promise of them all.

Cole snatched his cell from the nightstand, checked the time on his clock: 3:00 a.m.

He answered it with just one word: "Deborah."

Her garbled voice was fast and difficult to understand.

"Slow down," he said calmly. "Take it nice and steady."

"I hear noises," she said. "I think somebody is trying to get in."

"Where's your brother?"

Her silence was the answer she clearly didn't want to give.

"You're alone in the house, aren't you?" he asked as

his irritation at her obstinacy was quickly replaced by concern for her well-being.

"Yes."

He grabbed his keys from the dresser and pulled on a sweater.

"What do you hear?" he asked.

"It sounds like someone is turning a key in the lock of the front door, but the chain lock is stopping it from opening." She gave a cry. "How could they have a key?"

"Did you go downstairs?"

"No."

He slipped his feet into sneakers and holstered his gun. "Good. Stay out of sight until I get there. I can reach you quicker than the police."

"I'm sorry," she said.

He took the stairs in his home two at a time and headed for the front door. "What for?"

"I promised I wouldn't stay in the house by myself tonight," she said.

Cole broke into a run on the walkway, unlocking his vehicle with the button along the way. Was she really apologizing for breaking a promise? To him of all people. It made him realize what a good woman he had let slip through his fingers. And now it was too late.

"I'll be there soon," he said. "Just sit tight."

He uttered a prayer while racing to the house. He felt God's guiding hand upon him, giving him the strength to face up to his past so that he could help shape Deborah's future. If he was going to defeat the danger in her life, he had to accept her occasional harsh words, her resentment toward him and her instinct to push him away. It was his responsibility to take all of that and more.

He screeched to a halt outside her house. It was shrouded in darkness, and as he slipped from the driver's seat, the scent of calming lavender came to him on the breeze. Yet the calm was instantly broken when he saw a masked man standing on the porch watching his approach. Cole reached for his gun and the man began to back away, quickly swinging his legs over the porch rail and disappearing under the cover of the trees in the backyard.

Cole gritted his teeth and gave chase.

THREE

Cole scrambled over the fence that partitioned Deborah's yard from her neighbor's, in pursuit of the man in black. He landed in a child's sandbox and almost lost his balance as the silky grains slid beneath his feet, but he managed to stay upright, holding his gun close to his shoulder. The yard was small but with plenty of nooks and crannies and overhanging trees.

He stepped carefully out of the sand and stood in the middle of the lawn, turning in circles to scan the area, noting the patio furniture, a large barbecue beneath a tarpaulin and fishing equipment leaning against the fence. He was well used to working under the cover of darkness and his vision had been specially trained to spot movement that others would not detect. His last overseas assignment, the code-named Dark Skies mission in Afghanistan, had taken place under almost total darkness and had honed his skills to such a high extent that he often didn't need the infrared goggles supplied by the SEALs. Dark Skies had taught him to refine his steely focus, and for this situation it was the best skill he had.

He continued to turn in circles, certain the culprit was still in the yard, but confused as to why there was no sign of his presence. Then it occurred to him. He lifted his head to the branches of a mature sycamore tree in the corner. Hidden among the leafy boughs was the figure of a man, inching his way along a branch that hung over the next yard. The wood drooped with the weight of his body, and his position looked precarious.

Cole raised his gun. "I'd strongly advise you to stay right where you are, sir," he called. "I can hit a target a lot smaller than you with my eyes closed."

The man froze, gripping the branch tightly with his arms and legs. The bough continued to bend, creaking loudly.

Suddenly, the yard was flooded with light, and a man's voice boomed through the night. "Who's there?" Cole heard the click of a gun's safety catch, and the voice said, "Drop your weapon!"

Cole could see the home's occupant in his peripheral vision, but he didn't take his eyes off the man tucked away in the branches of the sycamore tree. The house owner was wearing a robe tied at his bulging waist and white socks. And he was holding a black handgun out front, using both hands to steady his grip. He looked scared.

"My name is Cole Strachan," Cole called out, not turning from his position. "I'm a retired navy SEAL. I live on Franklin Street and I'm here because of an attempted break-in at a neighboring house. I have my weapon trained on the suspect, who's hiding in a tree in your yard."

The man stepped out onto his deck, continuing to hold his gun defensively. "I don't know you, mister," he said. "And I don't care who you are. I just want you outta my yard." He called behind him. "Carol, call the police, honey. Right away."

"Yes," Cole said with force. "Please call the police. I'll stay here until they arrive." He saw the man in the tree inch closer to the edge. The creaking grew louder.

"Stay where you are," Cole called again, emphasizing each word. The man froze.

Cole felt the tension of the situation mount as the seconds ticked by and the standoff continued. With a gun trained on his back, he knew that firing his weapon would be dangerous and likely to result in him being shot by the petrified owner of the house. Scared people and guns were an explosive combination.

The man in the tree started to move again and the wood gave way with a mighty snap as the branch cracked and splintered beneath the weight. The masked man fell, still clinging to the broken branch, and landed on the other side of the fence. He bellowed as his body smacked hard on the ground. The owner of the house raised his gun into the air and shot a bullet into the sky, sending Cole instinctively diving to the grass. He tasted the soft earth in his mouth and spat on the ground.

"I hear the police sirens," the man shouted. His voice was wavering. His anxiety level was high, and Cole certainly didn't want to add to it. The man already had discharged his weapon once and would easily do it again if spooked.

Cole raised his head from the ground, trying to listen for sounds coming from the other side of the fence. He heard the groans of a winded man hauling himself to his feet and running away. He couldn't believe he was so close to Deborah's attacker, yet unable to apprehend him. He clenched his jaw in frustration.

"Next time," he muttered under his breath. "I'll be ready."

Deborah watched from her bedroom window while Cole spoke with police officers in her neighbor's yard. Her pulse was returning to normal as the surge of adrenaline began to wear off. She'd woken up two hours ago to the sound of a key turning in her front door. She'd sat upright in bed, immediately reaching for the card she'd so carefully placed on her nightstand before going to sleep. Cole's voice on the end of the line had instilled a feeling of reassurance and safety, but she wished she hadn't needed him to take control of this situation. She didn't want anything from him, least of all his protection. She'd learned to get by without the love and security he had once offered. And she no longer wanted it.

After first taking her statement, the officers then spoke at length to Cole and her neighbor Mr. Rafferty. They then went to inspect the tree in Mr. Rafferty's yard, where a large branch had been severed from its trunk. The four men stood together, discussing the incident, while Deborah had chosen to retreat to the safety of her bedroom. She watched Cole and Mr. Rafferty shake hands, and the officers made their way back to their vehicle. She lost sight of the four figures as they walked to the street together. Then Cole reemerged in her backyard, squatting down to inspect the footprints left in the dew on the lawn. They snaked around in circles as if the man had been uncertain which way to go. She reached for a sweatshirt and pulled it over her head, feeling her curls straining to break free from the hood. Despite two nights of poor sleep, she was wide-awake and alert, but she knew that exhaustion would hit like a ton of bricks later on.

She slipped her feet into sneakers and walked down the stairs, taking deep, steadying breaths. Every time she spoke to Cole, her stomach rebelled, refusing to be calm and still. It was maddening, but she was powerless to stop it.

"Hi," she said, walking out onto the porch.

Cole instantly stopped what he was doing and stood up to give her his full attention.

"Are you okay, Debs?" he asked.

She nodded, but it was a lie. And she reckoned he knew it.

"The guy hasn't been found, but the police have filed a report," he said. "The officers said they'll send extra patrol cars to the area." He shrugged his shoulders. "But they're treating it as a minor misdemeanor."

"I told them about the attack in the parking lot, but they said the exact same thing as Frank—a probable mugging."

"It's up to us to prove these incidents are all connected," Cole said. "And that means you have to let me in a bit more. It's way too dangerous for you to be here alone, especially now that we know somebody's been casing the house. We need a better plan."

Deborah shivered in the freshness of the breaking dawn. Cole wore a blue sweatshirt, spotted with mud stains. His hands were stained with dirt and his hair contained pieces of moss or grass, easily seen against the light red color of the strands.

"You look like you had a fight with a tree," she said, ignoring his statement.

"Yeah," he said. "It was something like that."

"You want some breakfast?" she asked, knowing she should reward Cole for his efforts. "You certainly earned it."

"Sure," he said. "Give me a few minutes to finish up here."

She turned and opened the screen door to go inside.

"Deborah," he called.

She turned back.

"We need to talk about your safety," he said gently.

"I know you don't want to face it, but you're in serious danger. Someone is clearly targeting you, and he won't go away unless we unmask him."

She looked at Cole standing on her lawn, hands resting lightly on his hips, his face a perfect expression of concern. He was right. She needed to act decisively.

"I'm going to the hospital today to talk to Frank," she said firmly. "If he won't call the police to investigate the possibility of drug tampering in the unit, then I will." She crossed her arms over her chest. "This has gone far enough."

Cole gave her a broad smile. "I knew you'd find your inner strength," he said. "I'm glad to see you're still as feisty as ever."

She drew herself up to her full height. "You ain't seen nothing yet."

Frank's face turned pale, then red, then purple. "Absolutely not," he shouted. "I will not involve the police. We still have no conclusive evidence to suggest that our patients' drugs have been tampered with. All we have are theories and gut feelings."

Cole stood shoulder to shoulder with Deborah in the hospital room where Frank had agreed to give them five minutes of his time.

"I chased away an intruder on Deborah's property last night," he said. "We think he somehow managed to get a copy of Deborah's front door key, but the chain prevented him gaining full access. Now, why do you think someone went to the trouble of cloning Deborah's door key in order to get into her house?"

Frank was stunned into silence. He looked at Deborah. "I'm sorry to hear about this, Deborah. Do you know how they were able to copy your key?"

"I figure that someone took it from my locker at the hospital and made a copy before I realized it was gone," she said. A slight tremor shook her body at the thought of a stranger rifling through her belongings, or even worse, someone she knew.

"And have the locks been changed?" Frank asked.

"I did it this morning," Cole said. "The old key is now useless."

"But we don't know that this incident is related to the hospital," Frank said. "It could just be an opportunist or a random thief."

"Oh, come on, Frank," Cole said as his patience wore thin. "You know that Deborah was attacked by a man in the underground parking lot, as well. What else needs to happen before you wake up and smell the coffee? Deborah is the one person in the pediatric unit who's pushing hard for an investigation into the abnormal amount of kidney failures. The fact that she's now been targeted in three separate incidents isn't a coincidence. It's a campaign to silence her."

Frank fell quiet for a while, rubbing his hand over his thinning hair. "A run of bad luck doesn't necessarily add up to a *campaign*," he replied. "Although this sounds like a rather far-fetched theory, I'll consider contacting the police to ask for their advice."

"Please, Frank," Deborah said. "We really need your cooperation on this. I don't want to go against your wishes, but I *will* make my own complaint if I have to."

"I said I'll consider it," he repeated. "Although it may reassure you to know that we've had no more renal cases in the last twenty-four hours, and five of the children who've fallen ill are recovering well."

"But a twelve-year-old boy now requires a transplant, isn't that right?" Deborah challenged.

Frank nodded his head. "Dr. Cortas has put that boy on the top of the transplant list. As soon as a suitable kidney becomes available, the operation will go ahead."

Cole decided now was the perfect time to learn more about the medical staff at the unit. "What can you tell me about Dr. Cortas, Frank? He's new to the hospital, right?"

"That's correct," replied Frank. "He came here from Shoreline Medical Center in Chicago just six weeks ago. He's a gifted and brilliant doctor who is highly regarded by all those who've worked with him. We're very lucky to have him with us."

"Why did he move from Chicago?" Cole asked. "Was he running from something?"

"As I understand it, Dr. Cortas was simply looking for a new direction rather than escaping a bad one," Frank said. "His references were excellent."

"And what about Dr. Warren?" Cole asked. "What is her history?"

"Julie Warren has been at Harborcreek Community Hospital for almost forty years," Frank said, clearly a little affronted at Cole's probing. "She's been a dedicated and loyal doctor throughout her time with us." He crossed his arms. "If you're insinuating that our own physicians are responsible for causing the kidney failures of the patients in Pediatrics, you're barking up the wrong tree."

"We're talking about the lives of small children," Deborah reminded him. "Cole is being thorough."

"Yes," he replied, having the decency to at least look shamefaced. He looked Deborah up and down, as if realizing for the first time that she was wearing scrubs. "Are you working your shift today?"

"I am," she confirmed. "I want to be here helping rather than stuck at home worrying."

"Well, at least that's one thing we can agree on," Frank said, heading to the door to leave. "You're a good nurse, Deborah, and the hospital always needs your expertise."

As soon as he was gone, Cole took Deborah by the shoulders and turned her to him. She flinched under his touch and he was reminded of the years that had passed between them.

"Let's be very guarded today," he said. "I'll be here helping with the security upgrades. If we keep our ears to the ground, we might hear something vital. Keep an eye on Dr. Cortas in particular. He looks pretty agitated to me."

"He did look like a rabbit caught in headlights when we walked in together this morning," Deborah agreed. "But he must be under an incredible amount of pressure. It's bound to have an effect."

"That's what I love about you, Debs," he said with a small smile. "You're always willing to see the goodness in people."

Cole realized what he had said. "I mean…that's what I *like* about you," he said, feeling the need to backtrack.

Deborah gave a deep sigh. "We may as well get over the fact that this is going to be awkward. You and I have a history that we can't change. I'm willing to try to put the past behind us for the sake of the kids."

Cole nodded in agreement. He was glad that she seemed to be softening a little toward him. "I know our history is complicated," he said. "And I also know that my presence here is hard for you, but I want to try to make things better between us. I want to make amends."

"Cole," she said, looking him straight in the eye. "Are you asking for my forgiveness?"

He returned her gaze. "Would you give it to me if I asked for it?"

She didn't even need to think about it. "Of course. What kind of person would I be if I freely take God's forgiveness and then withhold it from others?"

He smiled. Her Christian beliefs were obviously still as strong as they had been in high school. It had marked her as different and gotten her teased often, but she'd always accepted the teasing with good humor and invited people to ask questions rather than mock something they didn't understand. He'd never once seen her lose her temper or become offended, and it was her strength of belief that had drawn him toward God. He only wished he'd had enough faith to appreciate the difference that a good, strong woman can make to a man's life. Cole could overpower somebody with his bare hands, but he could never understand the kind of quiet power Deborah exuded when she simply sat in silence. Her power went beyond the physical, and it matched his in every way.

"Thank you, Deborah," he said. "Your forgiveness means a lot."

"Forgiveness doesn't erase the past, though," she continued. "I wish I could just instantly forget how bad I felt when you ended our relationship." She snapped her fingers to emphasize her point. "But I try not to judge you for it, and I don't want you to suffer because of it. I want you to be happy."

"The ironic thing is that I didn't realize how happy I was with you until I ended things," he said with a dry smile. "I was too young and stupid to understand that twenty-year-old rookie navy recruits aren't the best source of relationship advice. By the time I plucked up the courage to beg you to take me back, it was too late."

She knitted her eyebrows together. "What are you talking about? You never asked me to take you back."

He dropped his head. He had never intended to tell her these things. It wouldn't change the way it had turned out. But once he started, he found he couldn't stop the words from coming.

"Three years after I broke up with you, I came back to Harborcreek with the intention of asking you all over again to marry me. I'd just successfully completed the SEAL training program and I'd grown up a lot during that time." He took a deep breath, noticing the look of pure astonishment on Deborah's face. "I went to your folks' house to find you, but your dad told me you'd recently gotten engaged to a guy called Brad. He told me to leave you alone, and to let you get on with your life. I went back to Virginia and tried to forget you. After another couple of years, I married the wrong woman, and the rest is history."

Deborah let out a quick breath and stood open-mouthed for what seemed like an eternity. "I got engaged to Brad two years after we split up, but I still wasn't over you. Thankfully, I broke it off before I made the biggest mistake of my life." She put her hands over her face. "Oh, Cole, if only I'd known you'd come back for me. I had no idea. My dad never mentioned it."

"He thought he was doing the right thing," Cole said. "Don't blame him."

"I don't," she said. "But things could've been so much different."

He put his hand on her shoulder. She didn't shrink away. "Things are as they're meant to be," he said. "That's what I believe."

She smiled. It looked forced and unnatural. "You and I were clearly never meant to be," she said. "Dad probably did me a favor in sending you away. There was too much water under the bridge to go back to what we had."

He nodded mutely, silently agreeing.

An air of sadness had descended over the room and Deborah shook her mane of hair, snapping herself back to the present. "Let's leave the past where it belongs," she said, smoothing down her scrubs. "There are sick children who need us to be vigilant on their behalf. That's more important than anything else right now."

He was glad the conversation was over. His chest hurt with the pain of memories. "Keep yourself visible at all times," he said. "If you feel threatened, call out and I'll come find you."

She turned and opened the door. "I hope that won't be necessary."

"Will you promise you'll ask me for help if you need it?"

She waited a second before answering. "Yes."

This was one promise he really hoped she wouldn't break.

Deborah was all thumbs as she took an endotracheal tube from its sterile package. She dropped it to the floor.

"Sorry, Dr. Warren," she said, reaching for another packet on the tray. "I'm not having a good day."

"Is everything okay, Deborah?" Dr. Warren asked. "You seem very preoccupied today. Are you sure you should be here considering the scares you had yesterday?" She took the clean tube from Deborah's hand and prepped it for insertion into the young patient on life support. "Frank told me about the man who tried to break into your house."

"I need to be here," Deborah replied. "I'm so worried about the safety of the children." She dropped her voice to a whisper. "I know the toxicology reports came back clean on all the children in renal failure, but my gut tells me that something bad is happening."

Julie Warren looked over the top of her glasses at Deborah. Her gray hair was wound up high in a bun, wiry strands pinned into place. "I have the same gut feeling myself," she said. "And I hate to point out the obvious, but this situation started pretty soon after Toby Cortas started working here. He's behaving very oddly. I've been checking all his diagnoses and drug prescriptions today, just to make sure they're correct."

Deborah was relieved to find an ally in Dr. Warren. "I've given Frank until the end of the day to call the police in to investigate," she said. "I'm constantly looking over my shoulder, terrified that someone will be there waiting to attack. If Cole weren't here watching out for me, I don't think I'd be able to carry on."

Dr. Warren arched her brows. "Yes, Mr. Strachan is an asset to the hospital at a time like this. And you should be proud of yourself, Deborah. Frank isn't an easy man to lock horns with, but you're standing your ground. Many of us have taken our concerns to him, but you're the only one who's been persistent enough to get through."

"Do I have your support if I call the police?" Deborah asked. It was important that she knew she was backed up.

"Of course," Dr. Warren replied. "Now, let's change this patient's breathing tube." She held out the device. "You go ahead, and I'll supervise."

Deborah took the plastic tube from Dr. Warren in her gloved hands. She sat by the child's head while the doctor removed the old tube from his mouth. With careful attention to detail, Deborah repositioned the boy's head and slid the tube into his throat, attaching the end to the machine that kept his lungs filling with oxygen. They both watched his chest rise and fall in rhythm with the machine's whirs.

"Nice work, Nurse," Dr. Warren said. "Expertly done as always."

The doctor picked up her medical files and walked out the open door. Since the suspicion of drug tampering had arisen, Frank had insisted on an open-door policy. Cole was out in the corridor doing some wiring work in the wall. Whenever Deborah turned around, he seemed to be there. She knew he was deliberately picking the jobs closest to her, and as much as she hated to admit it, it comforted her.

"How's this little guy doing?" Cole asked, stepping into the room and pointing to the small boy lying in bed.

"He's very sick with leukemia," she replied. "He was having lots of seizures so we put him in a coma, but he's fighting hard."

Cole held his screwdriver by his side and watched the boy for a while. Deborah saw his eyes take on a far-away look, as if he was being transported back to another time. She wondered if he was thinking about the loss of his own young son, Elliot. She felt compelled to try to say some words of comfort.

"Losing a child is the worst pain a parent can endure," she said softly. "I can't speak from my own experience, but I've consoled many parents in your position."

Cole didn't take his eyes from the child on the bed. "I've seen too many kids die," he said without emotion. "When I was in Afghanistan, I buried so many that I lost count."

"That's awful," she said. "I can't imagine."

Cole turned his eyes to rest on Deborah. "I admire

you for being able to work with sick children every day of your life. I just couldn't do it."

"It's not easy," she said. "Some days I wish I was anything but a nurse." She touched the sheet on the bed where the boy lay. "But this is my calling. It's where I'm meant to be."

"I guess our callings are totally different," he said. "After I lost Elliot, I decided that God didn't want children to feature in my life."

"And that's why you don't want to marry again?" She felt she was beginning to understand him on a deeper level. "That's why you don't want to have any more children?"

"I'm an ex-SEAL," he said. "I'm trained to take the lives of the guilty and save the innocent. If I can't save an innocent child from harm, then I don't want to be responsible for bringing it into the world."

Deborah put her hands on the bed rail. "The Kingdom of God belongs to those who are like these children—Luke, verse eighteen, chapter sixteen. The children you buried are in God's hands now, and in His sight they are made perfect again."

He smiled. "That's a nice thought," he said. "But I still won't run the risk of burying another."

Deborah pulled the medical chart from the bed rail and updated it to include her work. "I understand your choice," she said. "It's not the choice I've made for my life, but I respect your reasons."

She clipped the chart back on the rail. Cole had hardened himself against family life, and she felt sad for him. But at least it confirmed her assumption that they were not meant to be together. They wanted totally different things.

* * *

"Frank, I'm afraid you've left me no choice but to call the police myself."

Deborah pulled herself up to full height and crossed her arms in defiance. She had already anticipated Frank's response would be a negative one, and she'd assumed it would fall to her to do the right thing.

"I can't prevent you from contacting law enforcement, Nurse Lewis." Frank's formal tone let her know that he would be uncooperative. "But I believe it's a waste of their time and ours."

Deborah was suddenly almost knocked off balance by Dr. Warren and Diane as they came rushing past with a crash cart.

"Deborah!" Dr. Warren called behind her. "Cardiac arrest in room four. Please assist."

"Cardiac arrest!" Deborah repeated. It was the young boy whose breathing tube she had recently changed. "But he was doing fine."

She raced into the room to find Dr. Warren charging the paddles of the defibrillation unit.

"Clear!"

Deborah watched the boy's small chest arch into the air before flopping heavily back onto the bed.

Dr. Warren looked at Deborah. "Start chest compressions," she said.

Deborah jumped onto the bed. Going into autopilot, she straddled the small child to give her compressions maximum impact. She put the heel of her hand in the center of the chest and began to rhythmically pump the heart. She had done this many times before, but each time was wrought with emotion.

Dr. Warren checked the boy's vital signs. "He's back,"

she said with a huge sigh of relief. "Let's get him stabilized."

Deborah had barely noticed Frank at the foot of the bed watching their every move. "What caused this?" he asked.

"The endotracheal tube was inserted incorrectly," Diane said. "He wasn't getting enough oxygen."

Frank picked up the chart. "And who inserted the tube?"

Deborah felt her stomach turn over. She knew where this was headed.

"It was me," she said, lowering herself from the bed to allow Dr. Warren and Diane to stabilize the child. "You can see my signature on the chart."

Deborah put her head in her hands. She had inserted the tube correctly. She was sure of it. She exchanged worried glances with Dr. Warren, and the doctor gave a small nod, letting Deborah know that she knew the truth. Someone had taken the tube out and reinserted it incorrectly. But it was Deborah's signature on the chart, and the buck stopped with her. Everyone in Pediatrics knew that a nurse's failure to deliver an appropriate standard of service could result in a suspension, and this was a clear attempt to set her up. Someone wanted her out of the hospital. Someone wanted her out of the way.

Frank's eyes swept over the paper before rising to meet hers. "This is a serious medical error, Nurse Lewis. I'm afraid I have no choice but to place you on immediate suspension while we investigate."

FOUR

Cole carried Deborah's personal items in a box as they walked to his cargo van in the aboveground visitor's lot. Her eyes were red rimmed and her face streaked with the faint lines of tears. He knew there was little he could say to make things better. She had been wrongly accused, and he felt the injustice of it deeply.

He was on high alert as they approached his vehicle, scanning the lot for any signs of danger. Whoever was targeting Deborah had just upped his game.

"We'll clear your name, Debs," he said, sliding back the van door and placing the box inside. "It's obvious to anyone who knows you that this was a setup. You did nothing wrong."

"It's not the suspension that's upsetting me," she said, rubbing mascara from beneath her eyes. "It's the fact that somebody in the hospital is prepared to take the life of a child in order to silence me. Who would do such a thing?"

Cole opened the passenger door and ushered her inside. The dramatic scene he had just witnessed had unnerved and angered him. Frank insisted that he had no choice but to invoke a suspension and had defended the action by calling it *standard procedure*.

Deborah settled herself in the passenger seat and clipped in her belt. "That child almost died," she said, closing her eyes tight. "How many more will suffer before we can expose the culprit?" She looked up at the hospital building. "And now I can't even be there to help protect them." She pulled her cell phone from her pocket. "I'm going to report this to the police right now. If Frank won't listen to me, I have no other choice."

Cole closed the passenger door and gave their surroundings one last check. There was a white truck in the corner of the lot that looked as if its engine was running, and a man in sunglasses and a baseball hat was visible behind the wheel. Something about the dirty white truck gave him a bad feeling. He stared at the vehicle for a while, noticed the mud obscuring the license plate numbers. The truck started to slowly move away, driving to the exit, and Cole watched it until it joined the highway, headed out toward the lake. He was glad to see it go.

He jumped into the driver's seat and looked over at Deborah, who was gripping the phone between her cheek and shoulder.

"I certainly would appreciate that, Officer," she said. "Please make sure you speak to a doctor called Julie Warren in the pediatric unit. She'll give you all the details."

There was a short pause. "My name is Deborah Lewis and I'm a senior nurse. Thank you very much for your help."

Deborah hung up the phone and looked over at Cole. "The police will pay a visit to the hospital tomorrow morning. I'm hoping Dr. Warren will make it clear that six serious kidney failures in three weeks is good enough reason to be suspicious." Her amber eyes squinted against the sun lying low in the cool September afternoon. "I just hope they find some clues, something that I might have missed."

Cole started up the engine and glided out onto the highway, heading for Deborah's home. Once there, he would delicately broach the subject of setting up temporary residence in her guest bedroom. She needed somebody providing round-the-clock protection. He was well aware that he was the very last person she wanted sharing her private space, but he just didn't trust anyone else to do the job right.

"Cole," she said, looking in the door mirror on the passenger side. "I'm sure I recognize that truck behind us. I've seen it hanging around the hospital parking lot. It's awfully close behind us."

Cole checked the rearview mirror. He saw the dirty white truck on their tail, close enough for him to see the bearded man wearing mirrored sunglasses in the driver's seat. The guy was wearing a camouflage vest over a khaki T-shirt. He looked as if he was dressed for combat, and his face was stony.

Cole pressed down hard on the gas pedal and the van picked up speed. The truck did the same. Cole turned sharply off the main road, and the truck made the exact same turn.

"In the glove box you'll find a gun," he said to Deborah. "Take it out and keep it in your hand. I keep it there as a backup." He patted his holster on the waistband of his jeans. "I have another one right here."

"I can't fire a gun," she said. "You know that."

"Sure you can," he said, reaching over her and opening the glove box himself. "Remember the day I took you to the firing range before I enlisted? You were a pretty good shot, as far as I remember." He flicked his eyes back to the truck and made another sharp turn, heading for open ground where he knew there would be few people. "You remember how to do it, don't you?"

"That was eleven years ago, Cole," she said, taking the gun in her hand. "It's a lifetime ago."

"There are some things you never forget," he said, recalling the way her hair had brushed his face as he'd helped her position the gun on target. The recoil had taken her by surprise and she'd looked at him with amazement at the power such a small weapon could wield. But her shot had been naturally good in spite of being a total novice.

She checked the bullets in the chamber and held the gun in her lap. She looked out the window. "Why are we here, Cole?"

He turned onto a dirt road, dusty and quiet, leading to a grassy area that overlooked the shimmering water of Lake Erie. It was a place they often had gone after school to be alone. He guessed that neither of them had been back in a very long time.

"It's time we found out who our mystery man is," Cole said, stopping the cargo van on the grass and turning it around to face the truck. "This is the end of the road."

They watched the truck roll toward them, and then it stopped about fifty yards away. Cole's vehicle sat face-to-face with their pursuer's, both close to the long drop that led down to the lake. Cole kept the engine running, waiting to see if the man would exit first. He didn't. The sun was shining directly onto the windshield of the dirty truck, sending a glare bouncing into their eyes. The lake flickered with millions of dancing lights as the rippling water caught the sun's rays. The scene was beautiful, but the atmosphere was not. All Cole could hear in the quiet afternoon was Deborah's rapid breathing. Her knuckles had grown white with the force of her grip around the handle of the gun.

"What do we do now?" Deborah asked. "Is this a standoff to see who breaks first?"

"Stay down," Cole said, pressing her shoulder. "Shoot only if you have to."

He slid down his window and then opened the door as wide as it could go. Slipping out of the van, he used the door as a shield and the open window as a stable base for his hands. He pointed the barrel of his gun at the stationary truck.

"Get out of the vehicle," he shouted to the man, who sat unmoving behind the wheel. "And nobody will get hurt. Let's talk."

The man remained impassive but revved his engine hard. The old truck rattled and shook with the excessive force. The gesture was aggressive. This guy was angry, and he wanted them to know it. In the next moment, Cole saw the barrel of a shotgun slide slowly out the window of the truck. With lightning reflexes, he jumped back into the driver's seat and slammed the door shut.

Deborah saw the shotgun, gave a small yelp and slid her body down into the foot well, out of sight. Cole narrowed his eyes at the truck. Now it really was a standoff. While he deliberated his next move, a high-pitched scream filled the air. It wasn't a scream of fear, but the sound of a playing child. His eyes shot to the edge of the cliff, and three small faces emerged from the grass.

He was surprised. "How on earth did they get there?"

Deborah's face was pale as she crawled onto the seat. "Steps were built down to the water a few years back," she said. "I totally forgot."

The three children squealed and ran in circles on some pebbles, picking them up and throwing them over the edge. A couple appeared shortly after and admonished them, taking their hands and beginning to walk along the edge of the embankment. The scene of happy family life sat uneasily alongside the danger of the developing situation.

The presence of the family clearly had an immediate effect on the driver of the truck. His wheels spun on the ground, sending smoke billowing into the air, and he sped from the area in a hurry. Cole watched the truck's rear end bouncing high into the air as it hit rocks with force. Within a few moments he was gone, leaving just wispy traces of his presence floating on the breeze.

"Did you see the license plate?" Cole asked.

Deborah unfolded her legs from beneath her and sat fully in the seat. He put a reassuring hand on her shoulder to let her know she was safe.

"I couldn't make it out behind the dirt," she answered.

"Neither could I," he said. "But I did manage to see the state where it was registered."

"What was it?"

"Illinois. I think our next avenue of investigation should be Shoreline Medical Center in Chicago."

Deborah sat in her favorite armchair with a mug of steaming hot tea. She used both hands to steady the cup. Her fingers felt cold, and her muscles ached with the kind of discomfort that only comes from pent-up fear. Today had started off bad and had quickly gotten a whole lot worse.

Cole was on the phone in the kitchen speaking to a doctor at the hospital in Chicago where Dr. Cortas had worked prior to his appointment at Harborcreek. She heard his low, rich voice echo through the house. Male voices were rarely heard in her small home, but she had often dreamed of a time when she would share this space with a husband—someone who would wake her in the morning with a cup of coffee, someone who would run her a hot bath after a long shift, someone who would one day convert the guest room into a nursery. Working with children had made her yearn for a child of her own, and on this matter, she and Cole couldn't be more different. Whereas they once seemed a perfect match, they were now poles apart.

Cole walked into the living room and sat on the couch opposite her chair. His attention was caught by a photograph on the table next to his seat—it was a picture of Deborah on graduation day standing proudly between her parents. Her mortarboard hat had refused to sit flat on her head due to her unruly curls, and her mom had inserted numerous pins to keep it in place. Shortly after the photo was taken, the hat had pinged off, sending her into fits of giggles. Cole's face broke into a wide smile, obviously remembering the fact that he'd been the person behind the camera who'd captured the happy moment. But his smile was as fleeting as the memory, and he slid his eyes from the photo without a word.

"I spoke to a doctor who used to work with Dr. Cortas at Shoreline in Chicago," he said.

Deborah moved her fingers around the cup, trying to warm each one. "Before we make any plans, shouldn't we call the police and report what just happened?"

Cole leaned forward, put his forearms on his knees and clasped his hands together, tensing his biceps. "I'm not sure what good it would do, Debs. We don't have a license plate or an ID on the suspect. The police would just write it off as a road rage incident. I'd rather trust my own investigation."

"But they might link the incident to the hospital,"

she protested. "If we can prove all these attacks are connected, the police might take us a little more seriously. If we do nothing, they won't even start looking for this guy."

"Those are all big *ifs*, Deborah," Cole said gently. "The police are visiting the hospital tomorrow, right? Let's wait until they've had a chance to uncover anything that supports your story. In the meantime, we'll continue with our own lines of inquiry."

"And what are they?"

"As I said, I spoke with a doctor in Chicago. His name is Alan Gorman and he's a former colleague of Dr. Cortas's. He was very reluctant to talk to me. He said he was bound by rules of confidentiality and couldn't divulge any details of Dr. Cortas's professional career at Shoreline."

Deborah felt her heart sinking. "So that line of inquiry is closed, then?"

"Not exactly. I told Dr. Gorman that Harborcreek Hospital has experienced a high number of children suffering kidney failure since Dr. Cortas's appointment, and he became very agitated. It was clear he was hiding something."

Deborah put down her cup, her interest renewed. "Did you manage to get any information from him?"

"He refuses to speak about it on the telephone. He says he needs to be sure we're not from a newspaper. He's agreed to meet us in person tomorrow."

"Where?"

"In Chicago." Cole rubbed his hands together. "We're taking a little road trip."

Deborah mentally did the math. "That'll take us a whole day, Cole," she said. "At least seven or eight hours."

"I know. We'll make an early start. Can you stand to be stuck on the road with me for that long?" He had tried to make the question sound jokey, but she guessed his concern was genuine.

"I think I'll manage," she replied, although she silently admitted that being in such close proximity to Cole would be difficult. Sometimes when he frowned or circled his shoulders in wide movements, she saw the old habits that she had adored a long time ago. Just the simple act of watching Cole run his hand through his hair reminded her of the happiness she had lost, and it made her heart ache. That sweet boy she had once loved was gone and had been replaced by an older, wiser and more cynical version of himself. Even thinking about it made tears rush to her eyes, and she was forced to blink them quickly away.

Cole saw the sadness. "You okay, Dee?"

She shot him a look. Cole's use of her pet name was unwelcome. Only her very close friends called her Dee, and Cole lost his right to be included in their number many years ago.

"Don't call me Dee," she said. "Please. Just stick with Debs, okay?"

"I'm sorry. Force of habit, I guess. You look a little emotional. Are you really okay about taking this road trip with me?

She picked up her cup and lowered her eyes to the tea. "Yeah."

"You sure?"

She didn't meet his eyes. "I'm not worried about going to Chicago. I was just thinking about old times… you know?"

He spoke quietly. "I understand."

She lifted her face. The way he was sitting with his forearms on his knees, head bent low, reminded her of the time she had seen him in the school principal's office receiving detention for two weeks straight. The memory made her smile and lifted her a little out of the gloom.

"Do you remember the day you put a mouse in the girls' locker room?" she asked.

His shoulders shook with laughter beneath his plaid shirt. "I sure do," he said. "I don't know what I was thinking. It seemed like a good idea at the time."

She laughed along, glad for the respite. "You got into so much trouble."

"Actually, it was all Josh Fenton's idea, but I was the only one who got caught." The smile on his lips lit up his eyes. "I had no idea that girls could scream so loud. My ears were ringing for hours afterward."

"I ran into Josh at the supermarket last week," she said. "He and Lori just had a baby boy…" She trailed off. She had ruined the memory. "I'm sorry, Cole. That was insensitive."

He reached out and touched her knee, brushed it lightly. "No, don't be sorry. I'm glad to talk about old times. I forgot how much fun I had in high school." He looked wistful. "I'd like to get together with Josh again. We were best friends at school, and I should never have let it slide."

"You just vanished," Deborah said sadly. "Once you got into the navy, it was like you disappeared off the face of the earth." She thought of their group of high school friends, still mostly living in Harborcreek and still as close as ever. "Whenever the gang got together, Josh used to ask if anybody had heard from you, but no one ever had, and eventually he stopped asking."

The pain this caused Cole was evident on his face. "I've got a whole lot of making up to do with a whole lot of people." He avoided looking at her. "I messed up."

"The boy I knew would never have turned his back

on his friends." She put her cup down on the table and leaned toward him. "What happened to that boy, Cole?"

He focused his bright green eyes on hers. "I forgot the lesson that the book of Corinthians teaches," he said solemnly. "Bad company corrupts good character. The buddies I initially made in the navy weren't exactly the God-fearing type, and I was led astray. I stopped going to church and started going to bars instead. When my superiors suggested I apply for the SEALs, I cleaned up my act. I'm glad that the SEAL training program gave me an opportunity to make the kind of friends who have moral standards I respect."

She listened intently, but she didn't speak.

"The men I served with in Afghanistan are the best friends I could have," he continued. "They all knew how much the Dark Skies mission affected me and, after losing Elliot and my marriage, they encouraged me to go home to Harborcreek. They said it was the only place I really wanted to be. And they were right."

"Dark Skies?" she questioned. "What's Dark Skies?"

"It was a SEAL mission to terminate the commander of an insurgent group in Afghanistan."

"And why did it affect you so much?" She wasn't sure why, or if, she wanted to know the details. "What happened?"

"I spoke a little bit about it at the hospital," he said.

She remembered what he said about having to bury the bodies of children. "You want to talk more about it?"

"Not really," he replied. "The evil acts of some people are beyond my understanding, and I don't want to dwell on them."

"Wow, Cole," Deborah said, sitting back heavily in her chair. "A lot has happened to you in the last ten years. No wonder you're different."

"It's hard to see the kind of things I've seen and not let it change you." He put one hand on his chest. "But I hope that I'm still the same person deep down."

Deborah said nothing. Cole certainly wasn't the same person he had been, but he had new skills and qualities that she was beginning to respect. He was tougher, steelier and less carefree—qualities he had developed in order to cope with the tragedies in his life and in his military career. She didn't blame him for protecting himself beneath a hard shell.

She suddenly noticed the time. "I need to get started on dinner," she said, rising from her chair. After all the effort Cole was making to look after her, she should show some hospitality. "Why don't you stay for dinner."

He rose with her. "Actually, I was hoping you would allow me to stay in your guest room until we find out who's behind these attacks. You need somebody with you at all times." He grimaced as though awaiting a negative response.

She had already anticipated the question and was mentally ready for it. "Sure," she said. "I'll get you some bedding and a towel after dinner."

He looked shocked, clearly having expected her to put up more of a fight. But she didn't need to. Her stomach no longer churned in his presence, and her body no longer shook when he touched her. She figured she could accept Cole's protection without it leading to anything more, and he would keep her safe from those who wished her harm. This meant she was over him. She was finally over him.

Cole awoke early, rising, showering and dressing before Deborah's alarm had even sounded. He had risen several times during the night to check the house, ensuring it was still secure. His body had been conditioned for sleeping in short bursts rather than one long stretch.

He heard the high-pitched beeps of Deborah's alarm clock. She shut it off and her footsteps padded across the floor into her bathroom. The pipes creaked as the hot water began to flow, and Cole started to prepare mentally for the day ahead. He needed to be coolheaded and alert, and not allow himself to be distracted by Deborah's presence in the seat next to him. He was finding it more and more difficult to be close to her without reaching over and touching her the way he used to—to brush her cheek or stroke her hair. He knew it was an automatic reaction, an instinct that was deeply ingrained even after all these years. There was no romantic connection between them anymore and no possibility of rekindling it, so he would simply need to keep himself in check.

He holstered his weapon and walked down the stairs to make a pot of coffee. There were many miles of driving ahead, and he had already contacted his Secure It team to let them know he would need them to continue the security work at the hospital without him. He had more important matters to attend to.

Cole poured black coffee into a cup and walked to the front door. Now was a good time to prep his cargo van and check it over before the journey. He opened the door and stepped out onto the porch. His foot made contact with something soft and squishy. He looked down. On the wooden deck was a teddy bear, brown and fluffy with a red ribbon tied around the neck. It had been mutilated, ripped to reveal the white stuffing inside. He reached down to pick up the bear, feeling the soft innards push against his hand. The eyes of the bear had been gouged and one was missing. The other hung by a single thread. This was a message intended to strike fear into Deborah.

Cole stepped back into the house and shut the door behind him. Then he heard Deborah's footsteps on the stairs and tried to hide the stuffed toy behind his back, but she was too quick for him.

"What's that?" she said, reaching out and touching his shoulder to try to turn him around. "What are you hiding?"

He brought the damaged bear out front. "Don't read too much into it, Debs," he said. "Somebody is trying to play with your mind."

"Was this left on the doorstep?" she asked, holding her hand over her mouth in shock. "What does it mean?"

He put the bear and his coffee cup on the table in the hallway. "It means nothing." He reached out to take her in his arms but she stepped away. "It's an attempt to scare you off."

"Somebody was here during the night," she said, raising her voice. "And we didn't know."

"I did regular checks on the house overnight, but this guy must've been real quiet." He put his hand on her shoulder. Droplets of water had fallen from her freshly washed hair, and her pink sweater was slightly damp. "But he didn't get inside and that's the main thing. Let's carry on with our day and get to Chicago. What we find out from Dr. Gorman could lead us to the person who's behind all this." He bent down to look her in the eye. "I won't let anything happen to you, Deborah. I promise."

"Your promises don't mean much, Cole," she said, turning away.

"Ouch," he said, putting his hand on his chest, where the words seemed to physically sting. She was scared, and he was bearing the brunt of that fear.

"Is there anything else out there?" she asked.

"I was going to do a thorough check before you came downstairs," Cole said, turning the handle of the door and pulling it open slightly. He quickly checked for other items. "I don't see anything else, but you should stay indoors until I've scouted round the whole house."

"There's something on the deck," Deborah said, pointing to the wooden slats on the porch floor. "There are specks of something red. Is that…" She gasped. "Is that blood?"

Cole squatted down on the carpet to take a closer look. "No," he said, inspecting the tiny red dots on the wood. "It's paint that's dripped from the door."

It was then he realized that a message had been painted on the door. Whatever it was, he wanted to see it before Deborah did.

"Stay here while I take a look," he said gently, holding the door close to his body to prevent her from seeing the words. "I'll only be gone a moment."

He slipped through the gap and scanned the yard for the intruder. It didn't surprise him to see only clear, empty space. The guy was long gone, having completed his task of terror. The bright blue sky and birdsongs promised a beautiful morning, and he didn't want to tear a scar across the day by allowing the darkness in. He steeled himself, closed the door, turned around and read the spidery, hateful words: *child killer*.

FIVE

Deborah was barely able to hold back the tears as she cradled the phone in her hands. "Did he die, Julie?" she asked desperately. "Please tell me he didn't die."

Dr. Warren's voice on the end of the line was shocked and full of concern. "What are you talking about, Deborah? Did who die?"

"The boy," she cried. "The boy we resuscitated yesterday. The one whose breathing tube wasn't properly placed."

"Ah," Dr. Warren said as realization dawned. "Yes, Deborah, I'm afraid he died during the night. I'm so sorry."

Deborah felt as if she were shattering into a million pieces.

"We discovered that he had a congenital heart defect," Dr. Warren said. "His death was nothing to do with his leukemia or the incorrectly placed breathing tube. His heart simply wasn't strong enough to sustain his life. He required major surgery, but he would never have survived the operation."

"So the lack of oxygen wasn't the cause of death?" Deborah asked.

"No, it wasn't. After we got his heart started again,

Dr. Cortas and I saw an abnormal rhythm that had somehow gone unnoticed, and we realized he had a serious problem. He was already greatly weakened from the leukemia treatment, and he just couldn't fight any longer." Dr. Warren sighed sadly. "We can't save every child, Deborah. You know that."

Deborah placed a steadying hand on the wall as the tears stopped flowing. She was dizzy with the exertion of emotion. She had assumed the words *child killer* referred to the boy she was accused of giving substandard care to. Somebody wanted the community of Harborcreek to blame her for the tragic death.

"I placed the breathing tube correctly, Julie," she said. "You saw me do it, right? I didn't mess it up."

"You did it right, Deborah," Dr. Warren confirmed. "I already told Frank the same thing, but he says he has to follow procedure. It's your signature on the medical chart, so the hospital holds you responsible."

"I think someone in Pediatrics deliberately put this child's life in danger in order to frame me," Deborah said, watching Cole walk past her with a bucket of soapy water. "And the words *child killer* were painted on my front door last night. I'm being framed for the death of this child."

"Oh, my!" Dr. Warren said with a sharp intake of breath. "Are you okay? Did you report it to the police?"

"I'm fine. Cole and I have decided to wait until the police pay a visit to the hospital today before we make them aware of what else has been happening. We really need the authorities to open an investigation into the drug tampering first."

"We've been told that the police want to interview all the staff this morning about a serious allegation regarding patient safety." Dr. Warren dropped her voice to a whisper. "Frank is livid that you went through with your threat to contact the police."

"I had to do it, Julie. I had no choice."

"And you did the right thing, Deborah," Dr. Warren said. "Nobody else in this hospital would defy Frank Carlisle as openly as you, especially without hard evidence. Even I don't like to go against his wishes."

"I don't need hard evidence," Deborah answered. "I know I'm right about this." She felt her strength returning as the shock began to wear off. "And if I have to prove it all by myself, then I will."

"I'll give my concerns to the police," Dr. Warren said. "I'm hoping that Dr. Cortas will do the same, but his nervousness gives me some cause for alarm. He's even more jittery today than he was yesterday."

"Leave Dr. Cortas to me," Deborah said. "I'll find out what he's hiding."

"I hope you do, Deborah," Dr. Warren said. "I have every faith in you."

Deborah hung up the phone and walked out to the porch to find Cole scrubbing the spiteful words from the door. She could scarcely bring herself to look at the faded writing, imagining someone being so filled with bitterness and resentment that they would write such a message. The water pooled on the deck, little pink bubbles lodged in the gaps between the boards. Her street was quiet and deserted, the residents all mostly still in bed at this early hour. She cast her eyes along the rows of cars parked curbside, imagining someone hidden between them watching her, waiting to strike.

Cole noticed her tension. "I've already checked," he said. "I scoured the entire street. Nobody's here."

"This can wait until later, Cole. We need to get on

the road if we're going to make it to Chicago by this evening."

Cole continued to scrub hard. "I wanted to get rid of this as quickly as possible." He looked angry. "Of all the people in the world, you are the least likely to harm a child. Whoever wrote this garbage is a disgrace to humanity."

Deborah was surprised at the force of his passion. She took a step toward him and placed a hand lightly on his back. It was the first time she had instigated a touch since he'd walked back into her life. He instantly stopped scrubbing the door and placed the brush back in the water, the muscles in his shoulders tensing under his shirt. She removed her fingers and he turned around.

"I've had dealings with the kind of people who deliberately hurt children, and they're monsters," he said. He took her hand. "To compare you to people like that is beyond wrong."

"It doesn't bother me," she lied.

He smiled. She forgot that he could easily see through her.

"Okay, okay," she said. "It bothers me, but I know it's an attempt to scare me off. And it's not going to work. If some lowlife thinks I'll be frightened off this easily, they don't know me very well." She looked at her watch. "We should leave. We've got an appointment to keep."

Cole emptied the bucket of water into the drain next to the porch. "You'd make a good soldier, Debs. You know that?"

"I've toughened up a lot over the last ten years," she said. "That's one positive side effect of getting your heart broken. It makes you stronger."

The smile slid from Cole's face. "If only that were

true for everybody." He reached into his jeans pocket and pulled out his keys. "Now let's hit the road."

Deborah looked at her white door where the words *child killer* had been scrubbed to a faded pink, barely visible after Cole's hard effort. He noticed her scrutiny. "I'll give the door a new coat of paint to cover the marks left behind."

"Thank you, Cole," she said. "I appreciate it."

"It's the least I can do," he replied. "I'm glad I'm here."

She found herself unable to return his words. She was grateful for all he had done for her, but she still felt uncertain about the future. No matter how hard she tried to shake it, there was a lingering doubt in her mind, a tiny hint of fear regarding his ability to keep a promise.

What if she couldn't depend on him?

Cole found that his cargo van ate up the miles pretty quickly on the interstate. Deborah was quiet in the seat next to him, seemingly lost in her own thoughts, no doubt about the message left on her front door. The words had enraged him, and he could still feel the aftereffects of the anger in his belly, where his muscles remained tensed and hard. It made him more determined than ever to hunt down the culprit and see him punished.

He glanced over at Deborah. She looked younger than her thirty years, wearing dark jeans and a pink Erie Sea Wolves baseball jersey. They had both supported the Sea Wolves in high school, going to as many games as possible. Seeing the name of his old home team stirred long lost emotions in him—feelings of belonging and camaraderie, feelings he yearned for again. They were emotions not felt since the Dark Skies mission in Afghanistan, when he would have gladly given his life for any one of his five colleagues. His thoughts turned to the one man in his unit who had not returned alive from the hot and dusty hills of the Afghan mountains. Ian Grey had stepped on a landmine, ending his life surrounded by his SEAL family.

The SEALs had been a substitute family for Cole ever since the death of his son and the end of his marriage. Yet he knew that a SEAL family was no substitute for the real thing. Even the toughest of soldiers needed the love of a woman back home to remind him that life wasn't always about bullets and war. That was why he'd gotten out when he had. Being a solider was a tough job for a single man.

"What did you mean earlier?" Deborah suddenly asked. "You said you'd had dealings with people who deliberately hurt children. Were you talking about the mission in Afghanistan? What was it called? Dark Nights?"

Cole felt his jaw tightening. "It was Dark Skies, and it's not something I think you'd want to know more about."

She shifted position to look at him. "It sounds like something you need to talk about."

She was right. He had a lot of unresolved feelings regarding the Dark Skies mission. But talking about them was hard.

"Go on," she prompted. "I'm listening."

He decided to relent and tell her the basics but keep the worst details to himself. "Anything I tell you goes no further than here, right?"

"Of course."

"Dark Skies took place four years ago," he said. "It was a mission to locate a terrorist group who had been classed as a top priority for termination by the local Afghan police. We tracked this group across the Nangarhar

Province, eventually engaging them in battle in the Tora Bora caves."

"What had they done?"

Cole rubbed a hand hard down his face. He felt the stubble of three days brush against his fingers. He didn't want to relive these memories, but neither did he want to forget them. They were too important.

"There are some men who don't think that girls should be educated," he said. "There are some men who think it's acceptable to use violence and aggression in order to make sure little girls don't go to school."

"And these men were like that?"

"Yes," he answered with force. "These men had destroyed at least three schools by the time the Afghan police asked for our help in tracking them down."

He saw Deborah recoil in horror. "You mean they bombed actual schools?" She put her hand to her cheek. "Empty ones, right?"

He wished she had never started this conversation. "No, these scumbags would wait for the children to go to school and then use rocket launchers to destroy them."

She gasped. "And that's how the children you talked about died?"

"Yes," he answered quietly. "Lots of children. And teachers."

"And you saw this with your own eyes?"

Cole focused on the road ahead. "I saw the aftermath." He remembered the numerous graves he had dug, the bodies pulled from the rubble, the cries of the people. "And I never want to see it again."

Deborah fell silent. He glanced over at her. Her eyes were moist and heavy lidded.

"It's really hard to keep your faith in God in a situation like that," he continued. "I just couldn't understand why children had to pay the price for the evil that exists in the human race." He shook his head. "Children are the weakest in society—the least able to defend themselves. The men who did that were the worst cowards I've known."

"Did you find them?" she asked with her full attention on his face.

A small smile passed over his lips. He took no satisfaction in taking the life of another man, but he took pride in protecting the lives of children. "We found them a couple days later hiding like rats in a cave. Men like these would never surrender, so they fought to the death. They were all killed."

"Did you lose any men?"

"One. He stepped on a landmine."

Deborah put her hand on his forearm. "I'm sorry to hear that, but I'm real proud of you, Cole," she said. "The work of SEALs is hardly ever reported, and we have a lot to thank you guys for."

He felt his chest swell a little. He had so often felt like a failure in Deborah's presence. It was comforting to know that she still saw some honor in him, despite the way he had dishonored his promise to her.

"SEALs don't fight for glory," he said. "We fight for justice."

"You talk like you're still in the military," she replied. "Like you're still fighting for justice."

"I guess I am," he said. "Those kids in Harborcreek Hospital aren't able to protect themselves, so it's down to us to make sure we fight on their behalf."

He saw her smile in appreciation. "I agree." She fell silent for a second or two before adding, "But I need to know that you'll stick this out until the end."

He felt his stomach plummet as he realized what she

was saying—she was questioning whether she could rely on him. It pained him deeply.

"I'm in this for the long haul, Debs," he said. "I know my promises might not mean much to you right now, and I have to prove myself, but you can trust me on this. I won't bail on you."

She wrung her hands in her lap. "Okay. Thanks."

She didn't meet his eyes and her voice was soft. It didn't take a genius to work out that she didn't believe him, not yet anyway. He had broken the most important promise already—not only had he broken off their engagement, but he had abandoned everything he had loved in Harborcreek, leaving her to pick up the pieces. Trust was earned, and he reckoned he still had a long way to go.

The skyline of Chicago rose from the horizon in the distance. They had made good time, arriving on the outskirts of the city at five in the afternoon, stopping only for a quick bite to eat and to stretch their limbs. Deborah had insisting on sharing the driving, allowing Cole to take a rest halfway through the journey. She hadn't spoken much, and Cole hadn't pushed a conversation. Whatever thoughts were going through their heads, they kept them to themselves.

"I called Dr. Gorman while we were at the last gas station and arranged to meet in a coffeehouse in one of the suburbs," Cole said, taking a turn from the interstate. "He doesn't want us to be seen by anybody at the hospital."

Deborah watched Cole navigate the busy streets, guided by the GPS on the dash. If he felt any anxiety, it certainly didn't show. His face was hard and determined. She wished she shared his strong nerves. Even though they were hundreds of miles away from Harborcreek, she couldn't shake the feeling of being watched. They knew that the white truck was registered in Illinois, and she found herself scanning the traffic uneasily, looking for signs of it.

"Relax," Cole said. "Even if somebody did manage to follow us, we're going to a public place. We're safe."

"I'm not worried," she said, sitting calmly back in her seat. "I'm fine."

Cole flashed a knowing smile as he pulled into the parking lot of a strip mall where a coffeehouse was tagged on the end. It had large floor-to-ceiling windows with good visibility. And it looked pretty empty.

"Good choice of venue," Cole said, unclipping his belt and opening the door. "I don't like dark corners."

Deborah stepped into the fresh air and stretched her arms, allowing her limbs to feel the freedom of the open space. The weather was much cooler in Chicago, with a dull, overcast sky, and a light rain beginning to fall. She pulled on her sweatshirt and raised the hood, shivering slightly and shoving her hands deep into the large pocket. Everything felt unfamiliar here, and she didn't like it.

Cole joined her side and stood close as if sensing her discomfort. She was glad of the reassurance, and they walked to the coffeehouse together, pushing open the large doors and heading for a table in the far corner where a middle-aged man sat cradling a cup in his hands. He rose when he saw them head toward him.

"You must be Cole Strachan," the man said with an outstretched hand. "I'm Dr. Alan Gorman. Would you mind if I saw some ID?"

Cole took the doctor's hand and shook it before stepping aside and extending an arm toward Deborah. "This is Deborah Lewis," he said, pulling his driver's license from his pocket and placing it on the table. "She's a senior nurse at Harborcreek Community Hospital in Pennsylvania."

"So you work with Dr. Cortas?" Dr. Gorman said, picking up the ID and inspecting it. He took his seat in the booth and slid the ID card across the table to Cole.

"I do," Deborah replied, sitting opposite the doctor. "He's a very difficult man to get to know. I'm hoping you can fill in some gaps about his past."

A young waitress wearing a red uniform appeared. She looked wearily at the teenagers in the corner of the coffeehouse. The young people were the only other customers in the place, yet they filled the room with excited chatter and noise.

"What can I get you guys?" she asked.

Deborah ordered coffees for her and Cole, hoping that the caffeine would give them the kick they needed after the long and monotonous journey. The waitress disappeared, shooting a glare at the teens banging on the glass window at the other side of the room.

Dr. Gorman swirled his index finger around the top of his cup and he appeared to be summoning up the courage to speak.

"Ready when you are, sir," Cole said, taking a good look around. "We're all ears."

Dr. Gorman took a deep breath. "I understand that some patients in Harborcreek have developed unexplained renal failure."

"That's right," Deborah answered. "Six children have become sick, one serious enough to require a transplant. We're concerned that Dr. Cortas may somehow be involved."

Dr. Gorman took a gulp of coffee and looked out the

window, where the rain had begun to fall harder. The light of the day was fading and the harsh strip lighting of the room highlighted the craggy features on the doctor's face. Deborah guessed that he was a lot younger than he looked.

"Dr. Cortas is an exceptionally talented doctor," he said. "He has dedicated most of his professional life to finding a cure for cystic fibrosis."

Cole held up a hand. "Remember that I'm not medically trained like you two," he said. "So it would help if you explained it to a layperson like me."

"Of course," Dr. Gorman said. "Cystic fibrosis is a disease that causes a buildup of mucus around the lungs, making it hard to breathe and digest food." He looked at them both with a serious expression. "It's a very debilitating disease, and those who suffer from it have a limited life expectancy."

"I think the average is thirty-seven years," Deborah said.

"That's correct," Dr. Gorman replied. "Dr. Cortas lost his uncle to cystic fibrosis when he was a child and decided to do everything in his power to find a way to beat it. Dr. Cortas himself is a carrier of the disease and this is why he chose to remain childless in case he passes it down." Dr. Gorman picked up the menu and pointed to a picture of a hamburger. "Imagine your DNA is like a recipe. You need everything in all the right amounts to make the dish come out right. In people with cystic fibrosis, the recipe isn't fully complete, so the body doesn't work properly. Dr. Cortas spent many years creating a drug called Cyclone that tried to replace the missing part of the recipe."

"So it worked like a cure?" Cole asked.

"Yes," Dr. Gorman replied. "Initial tests on mice

proved to be very successful. We managed to change the way their cells processed salt and water. It was heralded as one of the greatest breakthroughs in medical science."

Deborah touched his hand, sensing the difficulty Dr. Gorman was having recounting this story. "But something went wrong."

"Yes, it did," Dr. Gorman replied, looking up as the waitress brought their coffees to the table. They all fell silent as she placed the cups on the Formica table and walked away.

Dr. Gorman continued. "The Food and Drug Administration gave permission for a clinical trial to be conducted into Cyclone, so the hospital recruited twenty paid volunteers to receive treatment."

"Were these healthy people?" Deborah asked. "Or people with cystic fibrosis."

"They were healthy," Dr. Gorman replied. "The effects of Cyclone can easily be temporarily seen in the cells of healthy people, and the first phase of any trial is always conducted on those with strong immune systems."

"Are those volunteers still healthy?" Cole asked.

Dr. Gorman picked at a worn spot on the table with his fingernail. "No. In fact, one of them died and several others required organ transplants."

Deborah gripped her cup tightly. "Kidney transplants?"

"Yes," the doctor replied. "At first the trial seemed to be a success, and the subjects displayed no negative side effects, but after a week they all showed signs of massive renal failure. We immediately halted the trial, but the damage was done. A young woman sadly died before we could find a suitable kidney for her." He squeezed the bridge of his nose. "It was heartbreaking."

"What happened after the trial was stopped?" Deborah asked.

"The FDA revoked the license for Cyclone with immediate effect and required us to destroy all remaining vials of the drug," Dr. Gorman said. "And the hospital faced an investigation, resulting in a seven-figure fine."

Deborah began to see what might be happening to the children at Harborcreek. "Did you destroy all the remaining vials of Cyclone as promised?"

"I believed we did," he answered. "But Dr. Cortas could have removed some from the hospital without any of us knowing. He left Shoreline after the FDA investigation was complete. Although hospital procedures were criticized in the investigation, Dr. Cortas wasn't personally blamed, and he kept his license to practice medicine. He said he needed to make a fresh start someplace else. He was a broken man, and the hospital administrators gave him a good reference to start over with a clean slate." Dr. Gorman stared into his coffee cup. "Now hearing about the kidney problems in Harborcreek makes me concerned that Dr. Cortas is conducting unauthorized trials into Cyclone. But I can't imagine he would be so stupid."

"You said that he spent many years perfecting Cyclone," Cole said. "Maybe he just can't let go of all the hard work he's put in."

"Maybe," Dr. Gorman replied, looking into the distance. "But somebody died in testing this drug." He raised his voice, clearly remembering the difficult time. "She was a young woman with her life ahead of her, and we killed her."

The teenagers in the corner of the room stopped laughing and looked over in their direction. The waitress was midway through wiping tables and lifted her head.

"Everything okay, folks?" the waitress asked with a tense smile.

Cole flashed a wide grin to lighten the mood. "Sure, it's great. Thanks."

The waitress lowered her eyelids shyly and glanced back up to check he was still looking at her. Deborah felt her skin prickling with irritation, and she rubbed her arms to dispel the feeling. Cole could flirt with anyone he liked. It was none of her business.

Cole turned back to Dr. Gorman. "I understand that this must be difficult for you to discuss, sir, but let's keep our voices down."

"I'm sorry," the doctor said. "But there's not a day goes by when I don't regret what happened. I also worked on the Cyclone trial, so I'm as much to blame as Toby Cortas."

"Well, the information you've given us today is invaluable," Cole said. "But there's one point we can't clear up. The toxicology reports on the children in renal failure have all come back clean. Is there anybody who can supply a sample of Cyclone that we can take back to Harborcreek to compare against the blood samples from the children? I know you said you destroyed all the vials, but did you keep a small trace that would help us?"

Dr. Gorman shook his head. "All traces of the drug have been destroyed. The FDA ruled that the research into Cyclone must be totally scrapped. Our hospital honored that commitment."

Deborah ran her hands through her mass of curls, securing it with a band she found in her pocket. "Can you tell me what the drug looks like, so I can at least know how to spot it?"

"It's a watery liquid, pale yellow in color, stored in sterile, plastic vials about the size of your index finger.

The vials are opened at the point of use and decanted into a syringe or IV drip. It must also be kept in a refrigerator below thirty-seven degrees Fahrenheit, or it starts to degrade. It's a delicate mixture that requires careful handling. If Toby Cortas is administering Cyclone to your young patients, he'll know how to hide his tracks, but there will be pinpricks left behind on the skin, so I suggest you take a look at areas where you might not expect syringe marks."

"I can't do that at the moment, Doctor," Deborah said. "I'm currently on suspension."

"Suspension?" Dr. Gorman questioned, suddenly alarmed. "What did you do?"

"I did nothing wrong," she replied. "I was set up by somebody who wanted to remove me from the hospital while they continue their illegal activity. And now either Dr. Cortas or someone who's working with him is trying to stop me from exposing the truth."

Dr. Gorman looked anxious. "Have you experienced personal attacks because of this?"

Deborah felt Cole move a little closer. He was letting her know he was there. "Yes," she replied. "I've been targeted a number of times by a man who I think might be working with Dr. Cortas. He drives an old white pickup truck with an Illinois plate. Do you know who that might be?"

Dr. Gorman's eyes darted back and forth across the coffeehouse. "I had no idea there was danger involved," he whispered, leaning over the table. "I don't know anyone who drives a truck like that. Did somebody follow you here today?"

Cole interjected. "No. You're quite safe, Doctor. Besides, it's Deborah who's at risk, not you."

"All the same, I think I should be leaving now," Dr.

Gorman said, picking up his jacket. "I've told you all I can." He rose from his seat. "I hope you manage to put an end to the problems at Harborcreek Hospital. If Dr. Cortas is conducting further trials into Cyclone, you need to halt it before a child dies. This drug is highly dangerous and must be destroyed."

Deborah stood up to shake hands with the doctor. His face had paled and he looked spooked since she had mentioned the attacks. Clearly, he did not want to be drawn into her world of fear.

"Thank you, Doctor," she said. "You have no idea how much I appreciate your time."

He looked out the window into the parking lot. "I've taken a great risk in telling you these things," he said. "The hospital placed a gag order on all staff regarding the Cyclone clinical trial. I could be dismissed just for talking about it."

Deborah put her hand on his shoulder. "You were never here, Dr. Gorman."

He gave a smile of nervous relief and nodded his head, before turning and walking quickly away. Then Deborah sat in the seat Dr. Gorman had vacated and faced Cole with wide eyes. The tiredness she had felt on arriving in Chicago had dissolved, and she was hyperalert, ready to use this new information to their advantage.

"What now?" she asked.

"I think we should have a little chat with Dr. Toby Cortas," he replied. "Now we know his background, it looks like he might be using the children to carry on testing his drug. We need to confront him and give him a chance to tell his side of the story."

Deborah checked her watch. It was after six. "We won't arrive back in Harborcreek until the early hours of tomorrow morning. Should we stay overnight somewhere?"

Cole reached into his jacket and pulled out some money to pay for the coffees. "Let's hit the road and see how far we get. We can stop at a motel if necessary."

Deborah watched him pay the waitress, noticing the way the young woman behaved, coyly tucking her hair behind her ear and lightly touching Cole's arm when wishing him a good evening. Cole seemed to enjoy the attention and smiled warmly at her. The feeling of irritation bubbled up inside Deborah yet again, and she quashed it down, reminding herself that she had no emotional attachment to Cole. He was a part of her past, not her future. Besides, she was over him, wasn't she?

Cole strolled over to the exit where she was waiting and pushed open the doors, allowing her to step out into the chilly evening. He placed a protective arm around her shoulders and she didn't remove it. It felt like a shield in battle, and the familiar weight of his hand on her shoulder gave her comfort. She looked upward, watching the clouds darken, filling the sky with a promise of more rain. When she brought her eyes back to the parking lot, she stopped dead in her tracks.

Her gaze locked on a dirty white pickup truck parked at the edge of the lot.

Before she had time to react, a bullet streaked past her, slamming into the large window of the coffee shop. The glass exploded on impact, creating an earth-shattering noise that sent them both instinctively diving to the ground.

There was nothing she could do but pray for their lives.

SIX

"Stay down!" Cole yelled, pressing hard on Deborah's back.

He raised his head to look around. They were stranded in the middle of the lot with nothing but asphalt on all sides. Various cars were parked closer to the bigger stores, but next to the coffeehouse there was no cover except his cargo van about fifty feet away. He pulled out his weapon and lay on his belly, taking aim. Behind them, the teenagers from the coffeehouse came spilling through the doors, calling out to each other in panic, seeking escape from the gunshots.

"Go back inside," Cole shouted. "And call 9-1-1. Stay out of sight."

The young men made a dash for the door and scrambled back inside. The other shoppers who had been ambling through the lot suddenly vanished into stores and restaurants like animals fleeing a predator. The cries and screams of alarm faded as the lot emptied, leaving just him and Deborah to face the danger alone.

Cole began firing shots toward the white truck. "I see him," he called to Deborah. "Run to my van while I cover you. The keys are in my pocket."

She made no attempt to move. Her face was pressed to the asphalt, her hands covering her ears.

"Deborah," he yelled. "Go! Now!"

She shuffled on her belly closer to his side and retrieved the keys from his pocket. His vehicle wasn't too far away, but she needed to move quickly before his ammunition ran out. Otherwise, they would both be sitting ducks.

"Go!" he repeated more urgently this time. "Move side to side. Don't run straight."

He heard her begin the Lord's Prayer as she started her run, and in a second she was gone. The bleep of the unlocking mechanism on his cargo van let him know she had made it safely. All the while he fired sporadic shots to prevent the gunman from feeling confident enough to put her in his crosshairs.

But providing Deborah with safe passage had left him stranded in the open. He knew exactly how many bullets were in the chamber, and upon firing the last one, he jumped to his feet and sprinted like a gazelle for freedom. The bullets peppered the ground right by his feet, and he used all his training to evade a direct hit. But he sensed he was on borrowed time. There was nothing between him and the gunman but clear air. And the shots were coming ever closer to their target.

Then, just in the nick of time, salvation came. A second gun was being fired, providing him with the cover he needed to go the extra few yards to the safety of his cargo van. At first he thought the police had arrived and were discharging their weapons, but then he realized the bullets were coming from his vehicle. It was Deborah. She had taken the gun from his glove compartment and was shooting through the open window. Her aim certainly wasn't perfect, but it didn't matter. It gave him the protection he needed, and he silently gave thanks for Deborah's courage at firing a weapon he knew she wasn't comfortable using.

After reaching his cargo van, he hurled himself onto the driver's seat. "Get in the back," he said to Deborah. With no windows, the rear of his vehicle was used only for the storage of tools and equipment. "It's safer."

She squeezed between the driver and passenger seat and positioned herself on the floor between a set of specialist tools and a box of surveillance cameras. She pulled her knees to her chest and kept the gun close. He could see the shaking of her hand, and at that moment, he hated the man who was the cause of it. Deborah didn't deserve to feel this terrified. She didn't deserve to be hounded, in constant fear for her life. This had to end soon. And it was down to him to make it happen.

He reached across to the open glove compartment and grabbed a box of ammunition. As he reloaded, a huge burst of noise reverberated inside the van. Deborah let out a scream and jumped in surprise as dents began appearing in the metal, dotting the side of the vehicle like tiny footprints. Bullets were being pumped into the bodywork at an alarming rate. This kind of damage couldn't be inflicted by a regular gun—this was an automatic weapon, most likely a machine gun. There was no way he could defend Deborah against a machine gun attack. The situation was rapidly becoming like a war zone.

"I'm getting us out of here," he yelled, starting the engine. "Hold tight, Debs."

He pressed his foot hard on the gas, and the tires smoked and squealed in his haste to remove Deborah from the danger. He could see the gunman standing by his truck, gun on his hip, firing wildly in their direction. The look on the man's bearded face was one of pure anger and aggression, as though he was raging against the world.

The mall exit was within sight. They would make it out alive. Yanking the wheel sharply, he made the turn to take them out onto the freeway. He didn't see the police car heading their way at high speed, and he wasn't prepared for the impact.

Suddenly, his air bag deployed like a billowing parachute and his head was buried in the softness, muffling the sound of two vehicle hoods colliding together in a powerful clash of metal.

"Ma'am, are you all right?" The voice mingling with the smoke was female. Deborah saw a figure leaning into the vehicle from the open passenger door.

"Ma'am." The voice was now more insistent. "I'm a police officer. Are you conscious? Do you feel any pain?"

Deborah said only one word. "Cole."

"I'm right here," Cole said. "I'm okay." She could see him sitting in the driver's seat, rubbing his forehead. The air bag covered the steering wheel and his gun lay in the foot well where it had fallen from his hand.

He turned around, and she saw a smear of blood on his forehead. "You're hurt."

He brought his fingers up to the wound. "It's nothing. You're more important. Are you injured?"

Deborah eased herself up to a kneeling position. The numerous boxes surrounding her body had provided a good buffer against the impact, and she was tightly wedged between them, dazed and dizzy, but not hurt.

"I'm fine," she said. "Where's the gunman?" She felt panic rising once again. "Is he still here?"

It was the uniformed police officer who provided the

answer. "I'm afraid that the shooter took advantage of the collision to make a getaway. Thankfully, both my partner and I are uninjured, but we were a little disoriented for a few minutes. My partner is interviewing some people who saw the guy hightail it out of here right after the crash."

"No!" Deborah exclaimed in disappointment, reaching for Cole's hand to provide support as she climbed through to the front seat. "He got away again?"

"Again?" the police officer questioned. "Do you think you might know this man?"

"We don't know him, exactly," she replied. "But we suspect he's putting children in danger at Harborcreek Community Hospital just outside Erie."

The officer looked surprised. "Erie, Pennsylvania?"

"Yes."

"You're a long way from home," the officer said. "What brings you to Chicago?"

Deborah opened her mouth and promptly shut it again, remembering her promise to Dr. Gorman.

"It's complicated," Cole said, stepping into the silence. "Maybe we should discuss it at the police station."

"Are you sure you don't want to get checked out at a hospital first?" the officer asked.

They both replied in unison, "No."

It was clear to Deborah that she and Cole were on the same page. There was no time to lose in furthering their new line of inquiry. They needed to make it back to Harborcreek as soon as possible to confront Dr. Cortas.

"I'll ask a colleague to take you to the Jefferson Park station right away," the officer said. "Leave your vehicle here, and we'll get it towed for forensic analysis." She took a step back to inspect the damage that had been wrought on the bodywork. "This kind of machine gun attack is rare. This man needs to be found before he kills somebody."

Deborah stepped tentatively from the vehicle, catching sight of the crumpled, smoking hood of the patrol car that was firmly implanted in the front of Cole's cargo van. Despite the presence of several uniformed officers, she still didn't feel safe. Only when Cole joined her did she begin to feel calmer. This was the fourth time he had saved her from a truly terrifying situation. He was proving himself time and again. Maybe she could rely on him to keep his promises, after all.

A buzzing in her pocket caused her to jump with alarm. "It's my cell phone," she said, pulling it from the pocket of her sweatshirt. "And it's a hospital number." She turned to the officer. "I really need to take this call. I'll only be a moment."

She pressed the answer button.

"Hey, Deborah," a voice said. It was Diane. "How are you?"

"I've had better days. But I can't talk about it right now. Did the police visit the pediatric unit today?"

"Yes," replied Diane. "They were here for hours interviewing staff and patients and reviewing medical charts. I thought they'd never leave."

"So they've opened an investigation, right?" she said as a surge of relief rushed through her. They were finally making progress.

"No."

"You're kidding me," Deborah exclaimed. "Didn't Dr. Warren tell them how worried she is about patient safety?"

"Dr. Warren was taken ill this morning," Diane said. "She had to go home sick. It was so sudden. She looked awful."

Deborah put her palm on her forehead as her head spun. Dr. Warren was the best ally she had in the hospital: an experienced and respected doctor with the authority to make the police listen. If Dr. Warren had suddenly taken ill, it was likely a deliberate attempt to remove her from the hospital while the police were there.

A thought struck her. "Was Dr. Cortas there today?"

"Yes."

"Was he interviewed by the police?"

"Yes," Diane confirmed. "Dr. Cortas doesn't believe that the high incidences of kidney failure are anything to worry about. He told the police that it's likely to be a blip."

"A blip," Deborah said incredulously. "When the police find out about Dr. Cortas's history at Shoreline Medical Center, I'm sure they'll think differently."

Diane went silent for a moment before her voice came back in a whisper. "What did you find out?"

"Dr. Cortas's medical research has a history of causing renal failure," Deborah replied. "Can you please make sure you check everything he does, Diane? I wouldn't normally put extra work on a nurse in your condition, but I don't feel I have a choice. Dr. Warren was acting as a safeguard, but now she's sick. I only trust you to do it."

"What am I looking for?" Diane said. "What do you think he's doing?"

"I think he might be testing an illegal drug on some of the patients," she said. "He'd be using a syringe, so look for track marks. Dr. Cortas is very experienced and he may inject in places that are less visible, like the backs of knees or armpits. If you see any marks like that, call me or call the police. If enough of us make enough noise, the police will have to sit up and take notice."

Diane fell silent again. She seemed shell-shocked.

"Deborah," Diane said finally. "Are you sure you've got all your facts right? This is a very serious allegation to be making."

"I know. But all the pieces of the puzzle are pointing toward Dr. Cortas. As soon as Cole and I are back in Harborcreek, we'll be paying him a visit, but in the meantime, please keep the children safe."

"If you think it's necessary, I'll check all of Dr. Cortas's patients before I leave this evening. If I see anything bad, I'll call you."

Deborah smiled. "Thank you, Diane. You're a true friend."

"And you're a great nurse. Take care, Deborah."

With that Diane hung up the phone, and Deborah held the cell close to her chest, saying a silent prayer for her friend and for the children under her care.

It was now a race against time to make it back to Harborcreek. Would they return in time to prevent another child falling victim to a physician who seemed determined to cause them harm?

The police officer sitting opposite Cole and Deborah looked skeptical. He was a young officer, junior in rank, given the task of interviewing some of the witnesses to the shooting incident.

"So what you're saying," the officer said while writing notes on a pad, "is that you believe the gunman is working with a doctor in Harborcreek Community Hospital to poison children in the pediatric unit." He stopped to raise his head. "And despite clean toxicology reports, you still maintain that this rogue doctor is illegally administering a dangerous drug to them."

"That's correct," Cole replied.

"And you spoke to a former colleague of Dr. Cortas's today at the coffee shop in the mall that was subsequently attacked by the gunman. Is that also correct?"

Cole nodded.

"But you refuse to give his name." The officer sighed. "If you aren't willing to provide details to back up your highly implausible theory, I'm afraid there's not much I can do to help."

"I know it sounds crazy," Deborah interjected. "But we made a promise to the man we met today, and we can't give you his name. He already took a big risk in speaking with us. But I believe the things he told us are true. There *is* a drug called Cyclone that causes kidney failure in patients, and it's highly likely that the children in Harborcreek Hospital are being given Cyclone by the same doctor who used to work at Shoreline Medical Center."

"Even if this were true," the officer said, clicking his pen and placing it on the table in front of him, "the matter is out of our jurisdiction. You need to take it up with the Pennsylvanian authorities."

"Trust me," Cole said. "We're trying. But Deborah is being hounded by a man who drives a dirty white pickup truck with an Illinois plate." He leaned across the desk and emphasized his words. "Now that *is* in your jurisdiction, right?"

"We've put out a statewide alert for this vehicle," the officer answered. "And we've viewed the security footage from the mall. We only managed to get a partial reading on the plate, and there's no positive ID on the suspect, but we're interviewing all the people who witnessed the incident, and we'll do everything in our power to catch him." He looked at Deborah. "If this man is stalking you, ma'am, you should file a complaint with your local police department, and I'm sure they'll provide a robust response."

"I'm not being stalked," Deborah said. "I'm being hunted."

"Those are very strong words, Miss Lewis," the officer replied. "Do you mean to say that this man wants to kill you?"

"Did you see the damage he did to my cargo van?" Cole asked, moving his chair closer to Deborah's so that he could place an arm around her shoulders. "This guy was using an automatic rifle that looked very much like an AK-47. Tell me, Officer, why do you think somebody would fire a weapon like that out in public?"

The officer loosened his shirt collar. "We don't know yet."

"He was firing it on *us*," Cole said forcefully. "He intended to terminate Deborah." He noticed her flinch at his choice of words, but he needed to put his point across clearly. "And I'm guessing he was acting on the orders of Dr. Cortas."

The officer took a deep breath and picked up his pen and notepad from the desk. "I'll need to speak with my superiors about this." He stood up. "Wait here while I go find the sergeant."

The young officer left the room and Cole turned to Deborah. "We need to get back to Harborcreek," he said. "I get the feeling that the Chicago police won't be of much use, and time is ticking by."

Deborah closed her eyes, looking pained. She seemed exhausted. "How can we leave?" she asked. "This guy could be right outside just waiting for us to set one foot out the door. He's deranged, Cole. He doesn't seem to care about anything or anyone. He fired a machine gun outside a mall without any consideration for the innocent people who might be caught up in the storm of bullets. He's definitely crazy enough to wait across the street from a police station in order to take me out." She brought her hands up to her face as she finally crumbled under the strain. "I feel like an antelope chased by a lion, cornered with no way out."

"Hey," Cole said, putting his arms around her. "You have a way out. You have me."

"Do I?" she asked. "I know you've stuck with me this far, but I can't help but wonder how long your commitment will last. I know I must sound ungrateful, especially after everything you've done for me, but I just can't let go of this niggling little doubt that you'll cut and run at some point."

It hurt him to hear Deborah questioning his loyalty, but she had every right to do so. "I know you've had a hard time trusting me again after all the broken promises of the past, but please trust me now, Deborah. I *will* see you though this, no matter how long it takes or how difficult it gets. I'm here for you, and I won't let anything happen to you."

Deborah dropped her head forward, allowing her hair to obscure her face. "I want to believe you, Cole, but it's not easy to forget how you walked away from me once. What's to stop you doing it again?"

He tried to make her meet his eyes, yet she refused to look up. If only she could read his thoughts, she'd be able to see with certainty that he was a different person, more mature, more responsible and totally dedicated to her safety.

"I realize I have to make amends for hurting you,

Debs," he said, watching her clasp her hands tightly together in her lap beneath her bowed head. "And I'm trying really hard."

She lifted her head in a quick movement, sending her curls springing up into the air. "Is that why you're here with me?" she asked. A note of challenge crept into her voice. "Are you trying to make up for your past mistakes so you can wipe the slate clean?"

"No, not at all," he said. "I'm here because you need me and because I want to be." He touched her cheek. "And because I can't stand to watch you hurting like this."

He held her gaze for a few seconds, willing her to believe him. When he first had returned to Harborcreek, he'd wondered if he should try to atone for his past behavior, try to put things right, but he now realized it was futile even to try. He couldn't force Deborah to place her faith in him. The only way she would ever do that was on her own terms and in her own time. And to help her reach the right decision, he had to be unfailing in his commitment to her, living his life by example, proving that he had grown from a reckless, inconsiderate boy into a good, decent man.

"Okay," she said finally. "I'm sorry if I sometimes seem to be hard on you, Cole. I wish I didn't feel this way."

"Hey," he said, raising his hands as if she were holding a gun at his chest. "I'll take as many harsh words as you want to throw at me. I'm tough enough."

She managed to raise a smile, but it didn't come from the heart. "So where do we go from here?" she asked. "If you're thinking about leaving Chicago, you must have a plan, right?"

He pulled his cell from his jacket pocket. "You need

someplace to rest awhile. We also need a new vehicle, ammunition and a hot meal." He punched in the number of a person he knew who would provide all of those things and more. "I'm calling in reinforcements." He narrowed his eyes in concentration, working a calculation in his head. "What's the driving time from here to Pittsburgh?"

Deborah closed her eyes, mentally doing the math. "Around six or seven hours, I think."

When the number he dialed was answered, a familiar voice on the end of the line made Cole smile with joy.

"Hey, buddy," he said. "I'm sorry to spring a surprise on you like this, but I really need your help."

Deborah felt her head fall forward and snap back up again as sleep threatened to envelop her whole body. She was sitting in the police lobby awaiting the arrival of Cole's good friend from Pittsburgh. The clock had just reached 2:00 a.m. and the fatigue settling in her bones was impossible to resist.

Cole appeared in front of her carrying a steaming cup. "Here," he said, handing it to her. "Drink this."

She took the cup and sipped the beige, insipid liquid. She couldn't be sure, but she suspected it was coffee. Cole had added a generous helping of sugar, and she instantly felt the energy boost. He settled into the seat next to her and flashed a big, wide grin. She silently chastised herself for allowing her belly to flip. She wasn't supposed to react this way to Cole anymore. She thought she'd gotten past all that.

"Dillon will be here within a half hour," he said. "Not long now."

"Who is he exactly?"

"He's an old military buddy. We were in the SEALs together."

Deborah put her cup on the table to the side. "Did he go to Afghanistan with you?" She remembered the mission that had affected him deeply. "Was he part of Dark Skies?"

She felt his body tense up at the mention. "Yeah. He's still an active SEAL in Little Creek, Virginia, but I know he goes home to Pittsburgh on weekends, so he is able to come help us."

Deborah felt her head begin to droop again, and she let it fall onto Cole's shoulder. "Did the Chicago police say we could leave?"

"I had a long conversation with the sergeant before he finished his shift, and he was more than a little skeptical about our story." Deborah found it difficult to fully focus on Cole's words as her eyes closed and his deep, rich voice rumbled through her body. "He told me that the Erie Police Department didn't agree with our theory regarding Dr. Cortas, and they won't be following up that line of inquiry. They're still trying to track down the guy with the truck, but they won't speculate on his motive yet."

She moved her head against Cole's neck, trying to achieve a better sleeping position, and his stubble brushed against her face. It was comforting, giving her a feeling of security knowing he was so close. In her sleep-deprived state, she could almost forget that ten years had passed. She could almost forget that he had left her brokenhearted. But the little voice in her head refused to be quiet. The one that constantly reminded her to keep her distance, not to get too close to the man who had once held such power over her that she hadn't been able to eat for days after he left Harborcreek to join the navy. In the aftermath of their breakup, she'd lost twenty pounds. She must never relinquish that kind of power to him again.

"You're tired," he said. "Go to sleep and I'll wake you up when it's time to leave."

"I should stay awake," she mumbled, even though it was obvious that her body would give her no choice in the matter. "What if something bad happens?"

Cole tilted his head to gently rest on hers. "If this guy is crazy enough to come looking for you in a police station, then he'll be faced with a line of people waiting to take him down. And I'll be at the front of the queue."

She smiled. As she felt her limbs float away on a cloud of slumber, she believed him. She trusted that he would step up and take a bullet meant for her. But her mind was weak. Tomorrow she would probably feel differently. Bolstered by rest, the doubts would creep back.

But while her dreams were full of Cole's strong arms carrying her to safety, she was blissfully happy.

SEVEN

Cole tried to stretch his back while maintaining his seated position next to Deborah. She had been asleep for twenty minutes, resting her head on his shoulder. He felt her breath coming in soft, rhythmic puffs on his neck, and he was forced to keep brushing her hair from his face where it tickled his nose. She looked so peaceful that he dared not make any major moves in case she woke. The hard plastic seats were supposedly molded to be comfortable, but after only twenty minutes of sitting, his whole body begged to stand and be stretched.

Occasionally he closed his eyes and let his cheek rest on Deborah's head. Her mass of curls provided a spongy cushion, and the scent of her shampoo was like vanilla ice cream. He knew he shouldn't be enjoying this moment. The intimacy of the situation had only arisen from her desperate need to rest and not a genuine desire on her part to be close to him. He had been permitted back into her life out of necessity and nothing else. Yet it didn't stop him imagining they were both still nineteen years old, carefree and full of hope for the future. If only he hadn't been naive and reckless back then, allowing himself to be led down a path that promised fun and excitement but had delivered only heartache. He had no one to blame for his stupidity, and now he was reaping the rewards of his foolishness.

He checked the clock on the wall—it was almost two-thirty in the morning. His navy SEAL buddy would be here any moment and Cole was grateful to have such a true friend come to his aid. He closed his eyes and said a silent prayer of thanks. His life may not have gone exactly as planned, but God had ensured he made good friends along the way. Dillon Randall was a man who would never let anyone down, and it was a blessing that he was available exactly when he was needed.

Deborah stirred. He bent his face down and kissed her forehead. He did it on autopilot, forgetting that ten years had passed. His actions took him by surprise and he waited for her to wake and warn him off. But she murmured and settled her head on his shoulder, nestling into the groove between his collarbone and chin, pushing against his neck like a contented cat. He closed his eyes. Maybe in her dreams she loved him again.

"You look like a man who's enjoying himself."

Cole snapped his eyes open and saw Dillon standing in front of him, hands on the waistband of his jeans, legs wide apart and a grin on his face.

"I thought you said you were in trouble," Dillon said. "But seeing you like this, I'm not so sure."

Cole smiled. "You have no idea how glad I am to see you."

Dillon sat next to Cole, patted his friend on the back. "I got here as fast as I could," he said. "The police won't tell me anything about what's happened, but whatever it is, I'll help in any way I can."

Cole kept his voice to a whisper, wanting to give

Deborah just a few more minutes rest before they started their journey again. "This is Deborah."

Dillon raised his eyebrows. "Your old high school girlfriend?"

"Yeah," Cole replied. Dillon knew all about Cole's past, and the regrets he had about letting a girl like Deborah go. "It's a long story, but somebody wants to hurt her. My cargo van is riddled with bullet holes and I can't reclaim my wallet or ammo from inside until the police have finished forensic analysis." He shrugged his shoulders. "I have nothing to help me protect her. And that's why I need you."

Dillon's face turned serious. He was several years older than Cole and had taken Cole under his wing when he'd joined the SEALs as a rookie, teaching him how to harness his youthful enthusiasm. Dillon was a man of great experience, and he earned the respect of everyone he met.

"And she has only you to safeguard her?" Dillon asked. "She has no police protection?"

Cole shook his head. "The police haven't yet connected all the attacks, and by the time they do it may be too late."

Dillon ran a hand through his thick mane of dark hair, peppered with gray at the temples. "You look beat." He nodded toward Deborah. "And she's clearly exhausted. You need somewhere to go and regroup, rest and get the resources you need."

Cole put a hand on his friend's shoulder. "That's exactly why I called you."

"I'll take you back to Pittsburgh," Dillon said. "Once you're rested, I have an old car that you can take. It's not much to look at, but it's good. I'll get you both fed and watered, and then you can decide your next move. You can tell me the details on the way."

Cole felt a surge of gratitude to Dillon, whom he knew would put his life on the line for any of his SEAL comrades, even those who had since left the military.

Dillon anticipated Cole's next words. "No thanks necessary. We're like brothers, right?" He rose from his seat. "I can see how much you want to keep this woman safe. She must mean a lot to you."

Cole slid his eyes to Deborah's face. "She *did* mean a lot to me."

"My car is right outside," Dillon said. "Shall we wake her?"

"Probably not necessary," Cole said, lifting Deborah into his arms with one clean movement. She offered little resistance and tucked her limbs into her body, continuing to sleep soundly as he carried her toward the exit.

"I'll put her in your car and then go back inside to get my guns signed over," Cole said. "She needs to sleep off the shock."

They walked out into the cold September night and Deborah awoke with a start when the breeze hit her face. She looked confused, crinkling her eyebrows at Cole, realizing that she was in his arms, curled into his chest. She straightened her body, forcing him to place her feet on the ground.

"Are we leaving already?" Her voice was thick with sleep.

Dillon stepped forward. "Hello, Deborah. My name is Dillon Randall and I'm a navy SEAL colleague of Cole's. I'm here to help out."

Deborah looked him up and down. She wiped the sleep from her eyes and turned to Cole. "Are you totally sure we can trust him?"

"Absolutely," Cole replied with a smile. "You get two SEALs for the price of one."

Deborah stood in front of the mirror and towel dried her wet hair. Despite sleeping all the way to Pittsburgh, she had still been exhausted on arrival, so Dillon had shown her to a guest room in his home, where she'd continued to sleep off the dramatic effects of the previous evening. She was anxious and impatient to return to Harborcreek with their newfound information, but they needed to be well prepared for the task ahead.

Today she and Cole would confront Dr. Cortas. Maybe the doctor would crumble knowing that the secrets of his past had been uncovered. Just maybe he would do the right thing and confess to testing his illegal drug on the patients at Harborcreek, and give up the name of the man he had no doubt hired to dispense of her. She just couldn't imagine Dr. Toby Cortas turning to a hit man to silence her, but somebody was clearly prepared to go to great lengths to prevent this story from coming out.

Deborah noticed that Cole had placed a handgun on the dresser in the room, probably while she was sleeping. She picked it up, ensured the safety was on and placed it in the pocket of her hooded sweatshirt. Her impressive display of firing the previous night had obviously led Cole to believe that she was now comfortable carrying and using a weapon. He was right. She felt more confident knowing she could protect herself and was a little less reliant on him.

She walked down the stairs in the light and airy family house. Photographs lined the stairs. This was obviously Dillon's childhood home, and she saw an elderly man sitting in a recliner as she passed the living room. She smiled and said hello, but the man seemed to look right though her.

She found Dillon and Cole in the kitchen, making breakfast, even though it was past lunchtime. Cole smiled broadly when she entered the room.

"How did you sleep?" he asked.

"Good," she said. "This is a nice home, Dillon. Is that your father in the living room?"

"Yeah," he replied, pouring pancake batter into a pan, where it started to bubble and brown. "I stay at Little Creek in Virginia during the week and come home to take care of my dad on most weekends." He flipped over the pancake. "He suffers from dementia, and I share his care with my sisters. You're fortunate it's a Saturday. Otherwise, I'd be another four hundred miles away."

"I'm so sorry we called you in the middle of the night," Deborah said. "Did you have to leave him alone?"

"My sister came and stayed with him while I was gone," Dillon replied. "She left while you were asleep." He poked at the edges of the pancake with a spatula. "I can't really leave him alone. He has a tendency to wander off."

She sat at the table. "That's quite a commitment you've made to take care of him. Your dad's lucky to have such a loyal son."

"It's what we do for people we love, right?" he said. "We look after them, no questions asked." She saw him glance over at Cole, who busied himself laying the plates on the table. He had shaved and looked more like the fresh-faced boy she'd known in high school. The freckles that she had so loved covering his nose and cheeks were now a little faded, some having joined up in the sun, but they were still visible, dotted all over his skin like paint spots.

Dillon put a pot of coffee on the table. "I've got a car ready for you. It's an Oldsmobile that used to belong to my dad, but he can't drive anymore. It's pretty old but it's reliable." He grinned. "A bit like me."

Cole poured two coffees and gave one to Deborah. She took it gratefully. "We need to go confront Dr. Cortas today," she said. "And I'd like to check on Dr. Warren." She watched Dillon put his freshly made pancake on a stack already piled on the table. "We should leave soon."

Cole reached over the table and put his hand over hers. "Let's eat first and talk things over," he said. "It doesn't help anyone if we go charging off before we're prepared."

"He's right," Dillon said, sitting at the table with them. "The best defense is in the preparation. What do you know about the man who shot at you yesterday? What can you remember?"

Deborah pierced a pancake with her fork and transferred it to her plate. She had very little appetite but she knew she had to keep up her strength. "I'm pretty sure it's the same guy who attacked me in the morgue and in the underground hospital lot. He drives a scruffy white truck and he dresses like a soldier—camouflage pants, black boots, combat vest. I didn't see him clearly, but he sure knows how to handle a gun."

"He was using an assault rifle," Cole said. "Possibly an AK-47. This guy means business."

"A mercenary?" Dillon suggested. "An ex-military man hired to kill?"

"Perhaps," Cole replied. "But he doesn't seem military to me. His vehicle isn't well maintained at all. Hired hit men are much more organized and controlled." He took a big gulp of coffee. "I can't work him out. He's able to use stealth and surprise when he wants to, but other times he's reckless and uncontrolled. He was firing wildly at us rather than taking his time to aim correctly. I think he's either very angry or mentally unstable."

"Either way, it's not good," Dillon said. "And it's not enough information to identify him. Is that all you got?"

"I'm afraid so," Cole replied. "But when we go see Dr. Cortas today, I won't leave until he gives us some truthful answers. This has gone far enough."

"If anyone can get to the truth in all this, it's you," Dillon said. "I've never known a man as dogged as you. Dark Skies would never have succeeded without you."

"Dark Skies would never have succeeded without any of us," he replied. "We all played a part."

Deborah pushed the remaining piece of her pancake around her plate, feeling a sense of awkwardness, as if the two old friends needed time alone to talk. She heard a man's voice calling from the living room. It was Dillon's father.

"Can I go introduce myself to your dad?" she asked. "I'll see if he needs anything, and it'll give you two a chance to talk."

"Sure," Dillon replied. "Don't worry if he seems confused. He often forgets things."

She rose from the table. "I'm a nurse. I totally understand."

She turned and walked from the room, feeling both sets of their eyes on her. As she rounded the corner, she suddenly felt as if she was the new topic of conversation.

Cole crossed his arms in a defensive posture. He knew what was coming.

Dillon smiled. "So she's the real reason you wanted to go back to Harborcreek?"

Cole shook his head. "No." He knew Dillon could

spot a lie from a mile away. "Well, maybe she was part of the reason. I wanted to make things right between us."

"And is she pleased to have you back in town?"

Cole couldn't help but laugh. "Not exactly."

"Reopening old wounds, huh?"

Cole poured more coffee. "Something like that."

"She's very beautiful."

"She always has been," Cole said. "I was the most envied guy in high school."

"I see the way she looks at you," Dillon said, leaning back in his chair. "She still feels something."

Cole raised his eyebrows in disbelief. "Yeah, she feels anger and sadness and probably disappointment that I ever moved back to Harborcreek."

"Does she have anybody special in her life?"

"No. She was engaged to a guy a few years back, but she broke it off." He rubbed the back of his neck. "Which is probably what I should've done instead of marrying the wrong woman."

"But then you'd never have had Elliot."

"I barely had a chance to get to know Elliot," Cole said, putting his forearms on the table and bowing his head between them. "He was gone too soon."

"But he was still here on this earth," Dillon said. "Don't think of his life as a life cut short. Think of it as a whole life lived."

Cole lifted his head. "A whole life lived?" he questioned. "Are you serious? Elliot never lived a whole life. Those kids we buried in Afghanistan during the Dark Skies mission never got to live a whole life. They were cut down in their prime." He looked toward the door where he could hear Deborah's gentle voice talking to Dillon's father. "Your father has lived a whole life. He's an old man. That's the way it should be."

"Who says that's the way it should be?" Dillon asked. "Our time on earth goes by in the blink of an eye. The life beyond our world is unseen, so a life that ends sooner than yours simply starts the next journey ahead of you. You don't need to be angry about that."

"I'm not angry," Cole protested.

"Are you sure?" Dillon asked, looking at Cole's clenched fists on the table.

Cole loosened his fingers and spread his palms flat. "I guess I might be a little angry," he admitted. "It's hard not to be."

"I remember how it felt when we came across the bombed-out school in Afghanistan," Dillon said quietly. "It was horrible. Those girls who died battled against the odds to go to school, and they were brave and defiant in the face of evil. I've known plenty of soldiers who didn't have half as much courage as those kids. They lived the life they wanted instead of being oppressed and downtrodden into old age." He raised his eyebrows. "Now, *that's* a complete life."

Cole smiled. Dillon was a man of strong faith, seemingly unshakable no matter what atrocities he saw. "I try to give it all up to God," Cole said. "I know He prepares a place in heaven for all children who die, but I can't let go of the fear..." He stopped.

Dillon finished his sentence. "The fear that it might happen again. If you already lost one son, what's to stop it happening twice, right?"

Cole nodded. Dillon was always on the mark.

"So you think it's better to shut yourself off from relationships and be a single man for the rest of your life?" Dillon questioned.

Cole realized it must sound like a crazy plan, but it was all he had. "Yes."

Dillon let out a long sigh. "Nobody can promise that you won't experience loss and grief again in your life. You might suffer tragedies, or you might be given blessings, but you can be sure of one thing—if you don't take a chance, you'll never find out."

Cole felt his hands clenching into fists again. "I'm doing okay as I am. I don't need to take any more chances."

Dillon held his hands in the air. "Okay, if you say so." He jerked his head toward the door. "But if you let Deborah slip through your fingers all over again, you'll regret it."

Cole rose from his seat. "That's a moot point," he said. "Deborah doesn't want me in her life anyway."

Dillon started to clear the dishes from the table. "I think she's waiting for you to prove yourself to her. She's testing you."

Cole rubbed his temples. "I doubt it," he said. "She was really mad when she found out I'd moved back to Harborcreek. I can't do anything right." He picked up his gun from the kitchen counter and holstered it. "It's time we left. Thanks for the chat. I appreciate it."

Dillon picked up a black bag in which he had packed some ammunition from his own private store to replace the batch left in Cole's cargo van. He handed it to Cole, saying, "When people are angry, it's usually because they're hurting. Just carry on being there for her. It's all you can do."

"It's all I want to do," Cole said, pulling on his jacket. "She wouldn't last five minutes on her own."

"I'm sorry I can't come with you, buddy," Dillon said, putting a firm hand on his friend's shoulder. "But I'm just on the end of the phone if you need me. Take care of yourself."

Deborah appeared in the kitchen doorway. She leaned

on the frame, hands in the pockets of her jeans. She'd taken off her hooded sweatshirt to reveal her pink Sea Wolves T-shirt. Combined with her skinny jeans and baseball sneakers, she looked as young as Cole always remembered.

"Are we leaving?" she asked. "I'm ready to hit the road."

Cole turned to Dillon and embraced him in a bear hug, thanking him again for the help he had provided. Talking things over with his old SEAL friend had made him feel lighter and less burdened. It had made him realize what a fool he'd been to let old friendships slide in Harborcreek.

He began to wonder if he'd made a mistake in returning to a town where his social connections had faded and he no longer fitted in. He'd gone back to Harborcreek because it was the only place he'd ever felt truly happy, but was he simply chasing the glimmers of the past, trying to recapture an era now long gone? He had his family and a thriving business, but they weren't enough to make him feel truly grounded in the community.

He realized he was homesick for a town that no longer existed, at least not for him. And he didn't know what to do about it. He felt lost, and only his closeness with Deborah was giving him a sense of belonging. Deborah was more than just an ex-girlfriend who needed his help—she gave him community roots and fellowship. And the more deeply she allowed him in, the more he craved to share her homespun life.

Deborah was tense as they sat outside Dr. Cortas's house in the Oldsmobile. The car was at least twenty years old, but it had been well cared for and it allowed them to travel incognito.

Toby Cortas never worked on Saturday unless there was an emergency, so Deborah knew there was a good chance he would be home today. His car was parked in the driveway next to his beautiful wooden home overlooking the waters of Lake Erie.

"It's a nice house," Cole observed. "I'm guessing that Dr. Cortas isn't short of money."

"He never married or had children, so he only has himself to look after," Deborah said. "He's a very private man. None of us at the hospital know much about him."

Cole reached into the bag on his lap and pulled out a small black disc no bigger than a nickel.

"What's that?" she asked.

"It's a covert listening device," he replied. "Dillon gave it to me. I figured that Dr. Cortas might not be forthcoming with information, so we need to be prepared. If he clams up and refuses to talk, you distract him while I plant the bug somewhere he won't notice."

Her stomach swirled suddenly with anticipation and nervous excitement. Cole looked to be so calm and self-assured, yet she was full of anxiety.

He noticed her apprehension. "Are you sure you want to do this?"

"Of course," she said, rubbing her moist palms on her jeans.

He turned to her. "I can go in by myself while you wait here."

She contemplated that option for a moment before shaking her head. "No, I want to see Dr. Cortas's reaction for myself."

"Do you still have the gun?"

She pulled it out of her pocket. "Yes."

"Take it with you. Keep it concealed beneath your sweatshirt. I know you don't really want to use it, but it's there as a safeguard." He moved his arm to rest on the back of her seat. His hand hovered over her hair, almost touching it. "The way you held your ground last night with the shooter was incredible. You're much braver than I thought."

His words stung, even though she knew he didn't mean to cause offense. She was proud of the way she had proven herself to be strong and capable and not totally reliant on Cole. "Did you think I'd crumble at the first hurdle?"

"No," he said. "It was meant to be a compliment. You were never quite that brave in high school."

Now she was really irritated. "I think you have a selective memory, Cole. If I was such a coward, then why were you with me at all?"

His face fell. He obviously hadn't anticipated such a passionate reaction. "I never said you were coward."

"Now you're patronizing me."

Cole made a groaning sound and put his head in his hands. "I don't know how I manage to do it, but I seem to have an ability to make you mad at the drop of a dime." He raked his fingers though his hair. "I'm sorry. You were an amazing girl in high school and you're an amazing woman now. I chose to be with you because I wanted to be."

She swallowed hard. She so desperately wanted to stay angry but it was hard. She felt her defenses weakening. "Did you ever love me, Cole?"

He dropped his hands into his lap and turned to her. "Look at me, Deborah."

She kept her eyes trained on Dr. Cortas's car parked in the driveway. She concentrated on counting the bolts on the wheels. It prevented her from losing control of her emotions.

"Deborah," Cole repeated. "Please look at me."

She took a deep breath and slowly slid her eyes over to his. His pupils were large and focused, causing her to shrink back a little in her seat.

"I loved you more than anything," he said seriously. "I know it must seem difficult to believe, especially considering that I walked away from you so easily."

She remembered watching him striding along the shoreline of the lake, leaving her standing outside the café, too stunned to even cry.

"You didn't even look back," she said quietly. "You just kept walking."

His voice was as quiet as hers. "I had to. If I'd looked back, I'd never have been able to go through with it. I thought that once I was back at my barracks I'd forget about you." He sighed loudly. "I was wrong."

She didn't know whether these words comforted or maddened her. Where Cole was concerned, her emotions just didn't know which way was up.

"But don't for one second doubt the fact I loved you," Cole continued. He squeezed his eyes tightly shut. "I think coming back to Harborcreek has reopened old wounds that were best left alone." He gazed out the window. "Maybe I shouldn't have come back at all."

"It's a little late for that now," she said.

"I could go back to Virginia." He studied her face as if he was trying to gauge her reaction. "It might be better for everyone."

"That's what you do best, isn't it, Cole?" she said, feeling grateful at the return of her defensive anger. "When the going gets tough, you run away."

"That's not fair…" he started.

"It's totally fair," she interjected. "Promises are hard to keep and easy to break." She felt her emotional strength surge back. "When you were faced with challenges, you broke your promise without as much as a backward glance." She shrugged her shoulders. "And now you want to do it all over again."

"When I said I'd take care of you until this is all over, I meant every word." His voice was strong and resolute. "I'm not going to bail on you, Dee."

"I asked you not to call me Dee."

"Listen to me," he said, trying to take her hand, but she quickly moved it away. "We can either stay in this car and fight, or we can go see Dr. Cortas and do something positive to end the attacks on you. I'm here for the duration, and I won't let you down." He checked the bullet chamber in his gun. "Whether you believe me or not is irrelevant, because I'm not going anywhere. Period."

Deborah took a deep, calming breath. The heated exchange between her and Cole had shored up her defenses and hardened the soft spot she was developing for him. She felt better.

"Okay," she said, concealing her gun beneath her sweatshirt. "You lead the way."

The breeze blowing in from the lake was damp, and Deborah could taste the freshness in her mouth. She watched Cole approach the house with a watchful eye, attentive to his surroundings. The street was wide and empty of cars. No truck could hide here. Her anxiety level was high as she positioned herself next to Cole on the doormat outside the front door.

"Ready?" he asked.

"Ready as I'll ever be."

He rapped loudly on the door three times. Dr. Cortas took a long time to answer, but they heard movements inside.

"Who is it?" a voice called.

Cole opened his mouth to speak but Deborah jumped in first. "It's Nurse Deborah Lewis. I'd like to ask you some questions."

Silence.

Deborah and Cole exchanged glances. "Dr. Cortas," she called. "Did you hear me?"

She heard the security bolts on the door being slid across and it opened just a few inches. Dr. Cortas's face peered at them between the gap. He had large dark circles beneath his eyes.

He looked them both up and down before opening the door wide.

"Come in," he said. "I've been expecting you."

EIGHT

Dr. Cortas poured three cups of tea from a white china pot. Cole sat close to Deborah where she had perched herself on the couch, hands resting on her knees. Dr. Cortas offered them a piece of cake from a tray. They both waved him away. Cole looked around the tastefully decorated room with its gilt-edged mirrors on white walls. He felt as though he had been transported into an English historical drama rather than facing down a criminal doctor. He reached into his pocket and felt the small listening device nestled there. The leafy plant in the corner would provide a perfect hiding place.

"Dr. Cortas," he said, leaning toward the leather chair where the middle-aged man sat. "You know why we're here, right? So why not cut to the chase?"

Dr. Cortas looked pained. "I received a telephone call from a former colleague at Shoreline Medical Center last night."

Cole was surprised. "Dr. Gorman?"

"Yes."

Deborah was clearly surprised, also. "But Dr. Gorman told us he wanted our meeting to remain a secret. He was very anxious not to be associated with our investigation."

Dr. Cortas widened his eyes. "Is that what I am?" he asked incredulously. "An investigation?"

"Absolutely," Deborah replied. "I want answers from you. And I want the truth."

Dr. Cortas put down his teacup on a table beside him. The china clinked on the glass top and Cole saw that the doctor's hand was shaking.

"Dr. Gorman was a good friend of mine, and he felt uncomfortable about betraying my confidence," Dr. Cortas said. "So he called to tell me about your meeting. I understand he told you everything about my history in Chicago, and about my research into cystic fibrosis."

"We know all about Cyclone," Cole said. "And the death of a young woman on your clinical trial."

The doctor pinched the bridge of his nose and closed his eyes. "Yes, I live with the guilt of her death every day of my life."

"So why are you continuing to test Cyclone on the children in Harborcreek?" Deborah asked, her voice raised. "There are six children suffering the exact same symptoms that occurred in your clinical trial. Don't try to tell me that's a coincidence."

"I would never do anything to harm an innocent child," Dr. Cortas said, rising to stand. He leaned on the mantel. "I am not responsible for the renal failures of those children, but I agree that it's not a coincidence."

Cole was as confused as Deborah looked. "What exactly are you saying, Doctor? Are you telling us that somebody else is responsible?"

The doctor kept his back turned to them as he spoke, arms outstretched on the mantel. Cole could see his ashen face in the mirror. He looked pained as he spoke. "When I left Shoreline three months ago, I was devastated. I'd spent my whole professional career working on

Cyclone and the FDA ruled that it must all be destroyed."
He held his hands in the air, fingers splayed. "My entire
life's work gone in a matter of minutes. They wanted me
to erase my entire research."

Cole suddenly realized what the doctor was alluding
to. "But you didn't erase it all, did you?"

Dr. Cortas turned around. "I tried very hard, I really
did, but I couldn't bring myself to do it. I am a carrier
of the cystic fibrosis gene. It's why I never married and
had children. I thought I could resume working on Cyclone at some point in the future and make the formula
perfect." He clasped his hands together, and his knuckles
grew white. "I never gave up on finding a cure."

"How much of the drug did you keep?" Cole asked.

"I kept eight vials," he replied. "I smuggled them out
of the hospital before they could be destroyed."

"Oh, Doctor," Deborah said, rising to stand. "I can't
believe you were so irresponsible. You defied an official
order of the Food and Drug Administration."

"Yes, yes, I am aware of my failure," Dr. Cortas said.
"This is why I couldn't report the theft of the Cyclone
vials to the police."

"They were stolen?" Deborah gasped.

"Yes," he replied. "I kept them in a locked refrigerator in my basement. Shortly after I moved to Erie,
somebody came into my home. The refrigerator lock
was forced and they were taken. I have no idea how the
burglar entered, because there were no signs of forced
entry. I changed all the locks immediately."

"Was anything else taken?" Cole asked.

"Yes, some of my Cyclone research papers were also
stolen."

"That would suggest the thief knew exactly what he
was looking for," Cole said. "And yet you didn't report

it? You simply allowed this dangerous drug to fall into the hands of somebody who is now using it to harm the children in your hospital." He felt his temper rise.

Dr. Cortas wrung his hands together. "If I reported the theft of a banned drug from my home, I would be barred from ever practicing medicine again. Medicine is all I know. My life would be over."

"So you compromised the safety of others in order to save your own skin?" Cole said, not bothering to hide the vitriol in his voice.

Dr. Cortas sat down heavily in the chair. "Yes, I did. And I'm ashamed to admit it."

"When the children started falling sick with renal failure, you must have suspected Cyclone was to blame," Deborah said. "But you allowed it to continue."

"I recognized the symptoms immediately," Dr. Cortas said. "It was clear to me that Cyclone was being administered somehow, either through an intravenous drip or via syringe. If I had told Frank Carlisle of my suspicions, he'd have fired me immediately, so I tried to limit the damaging effects of the drug instead, and pretend that nothing was wrong."

"There is a boy on the kidney transplant list because of you," Deborah said. "We could easily have lost a child."

"And we still could," Cole said. "Whoever is injecting Cyclone into the children is still out there, free to carry on."

"Eight vials is a very small amount," Dr. Cortas said. "Whoever has it must be running low by now. There are only two remaining."

Deborah walked to Dr. Cortas's chair and bent down next to it. "Toby," she said gently. "You must report this immediately. You're a doctor. Your first oath is to do no harm."

Dr. Cortas gripped the arms of his chair tightly. "I knew you would say that. You're an excellent nurse, Deborah, and a person of high moral standards. I only wish I was half as decent as you."

Deborah looked at Cole. He gave her a smile of encouragement. She was handling this far better than he could. "We'll come with you to the hospital to speak to Frank," she said. "You won't have to do it alone."

Dr. Cortas nodded. "Frank will have to put the pediatric unit on lockdown until an investigation yields the culprit." He put his head in his hands. "What I don't understand is why anyone would do this. What do they hope to achieve?"

"Maybe they don't want to achieve anything," Deborah suggested. "Maybe they simply want to make the children sick so they can play the role of protector."

"Munchausen by proxy." Cole shot him a confused look. "It's the terminology we use when a caregiver deliberately makes a child sick in order to garner attention for themselves," Dr. Cortas explained. "Yes, that could be what's happening here, but it would have to be a member of the medical staff to make so many children sick."

"Frank said the toxicology reports on these kids came back clean," Cole said. "Would Cyclone show up in the blood?"

"Yes, it would," Dr. Cortas replied. "When the reports came back clean, I was mystified, so I carried out some tests using my lab equipment at home. The presence of Cyclone showed up quite clearly, so the hospital lab report was wrong."

Cole began to feel uneasy. Just how far did this sinister plot extend? He had assumed they were dealing with a rogue physician and a hired hit man, but maybe even more people were involved. "Do you think the lab reports were falsified by a technician?" he asked. "We could be dealing with a ring of people here. Deborah and I have already been attacked by a man who drives a truck with an Illinois plate…"

Dr. Cortas snapped his head up. "Is it a white pickup truck?"

Cole nodded.

"An old rusty one covered in mud?"

"Yes," said Cole. "Do you know who it is?"

Dr. Cortas laid a palm flat on his forehead and his color paled even further. "Yes, I know him. I suspect he is behind the recent threatening phone calls I've been receiving. I've informed the police, but they don't seem able to trace them. I also had some graffiti painted on my door, and a torn up teddy bear left on the mat."

Deborah gasped. "Me, too."

At this, Dr. Cortas seemed to grow in apprehension. "I think we should leave immediately for the hospital. I'll explain on the way."

Deborah picked up her pace, walking quickly to Dr. Cortas's car in the driveway. He was moving fast, seemingly anxious to get to the hospital. Cole lagged behind a little, acting as a guard, checking the street for signs of danger. Dr. Cortas had infected the atmosphere with an extra dose of fear, and her legs trembled with the sudden rush of adrenaline.

"Doctor," she called. "Slow down. Who is the man in the pickup truck?"

Dr. Cortas unlocked his silver Lexus. "His name is Harold Flowers. He's wanted by the police for making threats to kill me." He shook his head. "He's a very disturbed man."

Cole ran over to the car. "I'll drive," he said, taking the keys from the doctor's shaking hand. "You're in no condition to control a vehicle."

Dr. Cortas gave up the keys easily. "Yes, I think you're right. Just when I thought things couldn't get any worse, Mr. Flowers seems to have resumed his campaign of terror against you as well as me."

Deborah felt Cole's hand on her shoulder. "You ride shotgun," he said. He then turned to Dr. Cortas. "Get in the back, and tell us all about Mr. Flowers, because we think he's the person who attacked Deborah in the morgue and shot at us last night in Chicago with an assault rifle."

"Oh, dear," Dr. Cortas said, shaking his head and taking a seat in the back. "This is not good. Not good at all."

"Calm down," Deborah said, sitting down and buckling up. Dr. Cortas's sense of panic and alarm were filling her senses. He was scared, and she didn't need the extra fear burdening her already heavy load. "Take a deep breath and tell us what you know."

Cole pulled out of the driveway and headed for the hospital. Dr. Cortas's eyes darted side to side as he spoke. "Harold Flowers is the father of the young woman who died on the Cyclone trial in Chicago. He blamed me for his daughter's death and began making threats against me on the telephone and via email. One evening he turned up at my house with a gun, and I called the police. After that he had his gun license revoked, but he must have purchased weapons on the black market and then he turned up at my home again. The police arrested him and charged him with possession of illegal firearms and making threats to kill, but he skipped town before his court appearance." Dr. Cortas leaned his head against the window. "I thought that if I moved to a new town he'd stop harassing me, but I was wrong. He's back, and I don't think he'll stop until I'm dead."

"But why would he want Deborah dead, as well?" Cole asked, looking at Dr. Cortas in the rearview mirror. "She didn't have anything to do with his daughter's death."

"I don't know," Dr. Cortas replied. "Like I said, Mr. Flowers is a very disturbed man. His daughter was his only child and, after she died, his life unraveled very quickly. He lost his job and his home, his marriage broke down, and he ended up living in his truck." The doctor ran a hand down his face. "I think he may have lost his mind."

"Didn't he get compensated?" Deborah asked. "Surely the hospital was liable."

"He refused to take any payments from the hospital," Dr. Cortas replied. "He said he didn't want our blood money. He said he only wanted justice."

"Well, he certainly seems determined," Cole said, turning onto the highway to Harborcreek. "He attacked us last night with a pretty serious weapon. I think it was an AK-47."

"He was a gun enthusiast before his life hit a downward spiral," Dr. Cortas explained. "He had a very extensive collection of assault rifles that was confiscated by the police. He's probably got a number of contacts who would sell him guns illegally."

Deborah looked over at Cole. "It doesn't seem like this man has any respect for the law at all."

Cole met her eyes and lowered his voice. "There's nothing quite as dangerous as a man who has nothing left to lose."

Deborah glanced behind to Dr. Cortas. He had squashed his body tightly against the door and was clinging to the handle as if his life depended on it. She noticed that he had not secured his seat belt around him.

"Dr. Cortas," she said. "I'd feel much better if you put your seat belt on."

He didn't seem to hear, locked in his own world of fear. She leaned into the backseat and reached for the belt. Just as she managed to get her fingertips on the black strap, her body was slammed from the side, jolting her limbs with a massive force. The sound of metal on metal filled the car, and she felt Cole's body push against hers as a truck bore down on them, hitting them from the side. The windshield exploded with a huge bang, and Deborah covered her head with her hands to protect herself from the shattered pieces of glass flying through the air like diamonds.

"No!" she yelled as their car was pushed with great power across the asphalt. The other vehicles on the busy highway slammed on their brakes, and the sound of squealing tires mingled with the scraping of metal. Smoke began to fill the car.

"Cole," she shouted, trying to reach for his hand. She found his fingers and he gripped them tight, squeezing hard as the door of the car crumpled under the strain. Finally, the movement stopped and her body was still.

The car was filling with blue smoke, and Deborah coughed to rid her throat of the burning sensation trying to force its way into her lungs. She looked over at Cole, who was shaking his head, clearly dazed by the force of the impact.

As they tried to make sense of the confusion and chaos all around, Deborah saw a man slowly open the door of the truck embedded into the side of Dr. Cortas's

Lexus. She knew who it was even before she saw his bearded, craggy face emerge from the smoke.

She pointed and gasped. "It's him."

Cole reacted instantly, leaning over her and opening the passenger door. "Get out. Now!"

Cole pushed Deborah out of the smoke-filled car and quickly followed her. She fell to the ground and he picked her up, checking her for injuries.

"You hurt?" he asked, holding her close.

"No," she said breathlessly. She looked around. "Where's Dr. Cortas?"

Cole snapped his head around to the back of the car. The door was open and the seat was empty. Dr. Cortas was gone. Cole spun around, checking the vicinity for signs of the doctor. The traffic was in disarray with cars parked at awkward angles, drivers stepping out of their vehicles in bewilderment to survey the chaos all around.

"Where is he?" a voice bellowed through the clearing smoke. "Where's Dr. Cortas?"

Cole grabbed Deborah's hand and crouched down low, pulling her between the stationary vehicles.

"I left the gun in the car," Deborah whispered. "I need to go get it."

"It's too dangerous." He patted his holster. "I have mine right here."

Cole kept a tight hold of Deborah's hand and tried to find shelter. He needed to move her to safety. He peeked between the stationary vehicles and saw Flowers winding his way through the cars, a powerful rifle strapped on his shoulder. Cole knew that the firepower from his handgun was no match for an assault rifle.

"I know that you're up to your old tricks, Dr. Cortas," Flowers boomed as he walked between the cars.

"I heard you're now testing your wonder drug on kids in Harborcreek Hospital. And you've even recruited a pretty young nurse to help."

Cole saw Deborah's eyes widen in surprise. "Is he talking about me?" she whispered. Cole brought his finger to her lips and shook his head. He didn't want to reveal their hiding place to a man who would shoot first and ask questions later.

"You already killed my daughter, and I won't let you kill anyone else," Flowers continued. "You can run from me but you can't hide."

Suddenly, Flowers let out a burst of gunfire from his rifle. The sound of bullets hitting metal caused a wave of alarm to roll across the scene. Screams echoed through the air as people ran for their lives and ducked for cover. The gunfire ceased, but the panic continued to escalate, and Cole felt an urgent need to calm the situation down. He stood up. Three cars were between him and Flowers, but he was close enough to see the anguish and resentment etched on the man's face.

"Mr. Flowers," Cole called out. He felt Deborah tug on his pant leg, urging him to take cover, but he stepped away from her. "Please, sir," Cole continued, holding his arms up high. "Don't do this. Don't let your daughter's memory be tarnished like this."

Flowers turned around and faced Cole. The older man was wearing a bulletproof vest over combat pants. He had come prepared. "What would you know about my daughter?" he challenged.

"I know she died," Cole said. "And trust me, I know how that feels, but trying to avenge her death will only make you feel worse."

Flowers took a few steps toward him. Cole did the same thing, trying to prevent the grieving father from finding Deborah hiding behind the car. His only thought was to protect her.

"I think I'll be the judge of that," Flowers said with a sardonic smile. "It's my duty to stop Dr. Cortas before he kills again. He's already made lots of kids sick in a local hospital. And this time, he's got somebody helping him—Deborah Lewis. Where is she? I saw her in the car."

Cole heard Deborah gasp behind the car. The crowds of people had scattered by now, leaving an ominous silence in their wake. In the distance, he could see the small figures of people running, leaving behind the danger that Cole was now facing alone.

"Who told you this?" Cole asked calmly. "Because it's not true. Somebody is feeding you lies, trying to cover their own tracks."

"It's not lies!" Flowers bellowed. "I've seen the sick kids with my own eyes."

"We know you've been in the hospital," Cole said, keeping his voice low and even. "Did you attack Nurse Lewis in the morgue?"

"Yes, I did. And I'd do it again if I had to."

Cole heard the very faint sound of sirens heading their way. Flowers seemed too distracted to notice. Cole realized he needed to keep him talking in order to prevent him from shooting.

"Deborah Lewis is investigating the kidney failures of the children in the pediatric unit," Cole said. "She's been trying to help them, not hurt them."

Flowers narrowed his eyes at Cole and tilted his head. "You sound like you're trying to protect her. What are you? Her husband?"

"No, I'm not her husband, but I've known Deborah my whole life," Cole said, moving closer, putting more space between him and Deborah. "I can vouch for her honesty."

Flowers curled his lip in a sneer. "I know she was with you and the doctor in the car. Where is she now?" He jerked his head toward the small vehicle where Deborah was shielded. "Is she hiding there?" He took two steps forward, holding his rifle at his hip with the strap resting on his shoulder. "You seem pretty keen for me to stay away from that little red car."

Cole deliberated for a second. The sirens were still too distant. He had to act. Pulling his gun from its holster, he planted his feet wide apart and pointed it directly at Flowers.

"Stay where you are, sir," he said loudly. "I can't let you come any closer."

Flowers stopped in his tracks and jerked his gun to face Cole. "Do you know what rifle this is, sonny," he said with a tone of mockery. "It's an AK-47, capable of firing twenty rounds per minute. How many rounds can your itty-bitty gun fire, huh?"

Cole didn't move an inch. "The difference between you and me, Mr. Flowers," he said, staring him down, "is that I only need one bullet to do the job right."

Flowers let out a laugh. He looked down at his gun. "But you'd better make sure you kill me stone dead or else this Kalashnikov will put a few holes in you for sure."

Cole remained steadfast. "I'll take that chance."

Beads of sweat formed on Cole's brow as the standoff continued. The police seemed agonizingly slow to reach their location, probably because of the heavy, stationary traffic that was blocking the highway in all directions. He flicked his eyes to his left, where he could see Deborah huddled on the asphalt, head bent over her clasped hands in a position of prayer.

"Well, you got a lot of courage, I'll give you that," Flowers said finally. "I don't usually like to hurt anybody I ain't got a beef with, but if you insist on standing in my way, I'll have to take you down."

Flowers pointed the barrel of his rifle at Cole and let his finger hover over the trigger. Cole knew that his reflexes were good, and he also knew that Flowers wasn't the best shot in the world. He calculated whether it would be possible to dive from the bullets and fire back before being hit. He didn't want to fire first. This man was stricken with grief and not of sound mind. It didn't feel right to take his life unless absolutely necessary, but in order to protect Deborah, Cole would do whatever he had to.

"Don't do this, Harold," he called as a last warning. "There's still time to make things right."

Flowers shook his head. "That time has been and gone." He raised his rifle and prepared to take his shot.

"Stop!" A voice hollered through the air.

Both men turned their heads to look—Dr. Cortas was standing a few cars away, having risen from his hiding place behind a taxi cab. He was bloodied and disheveled, holding his arm awkwardly on his chest. It looked broken.

"It's me you want," Dr. Cortas said, snaking his way through the cars with a noticeable limp. "Neither Cole nor Deborah deserve to be hurt."

Cole kept his gun raised. Dr. Cortas was already injured, had no weapon and no means of defense. "Doctor," Cole shouted out. "Stay down. I can handle this."

"This has to end," Dr. Cortas said, coming to within a few feet of Flowers. "I'm so sorry about your daughter. I regret it every single day of my life."

"Not as much as I regret it," Flowers said, becoming noticeably emotional. "She was my beautiful princess."

Cole began to feel a surge of hope, watching the tears flow down Flowers's cheeks. It made him seem more human, softer and less dangerous.

"She was a wonderful young woman," Dr. Cortas said.

These words only seemed to remind Flowers of what he had lost, and his sadness turned to rage in a heartbeat. Without warning, he fired his gun with wild abandon, letting his anger overtake his body, crying out in anguish. Cole hurled his body to the ground and took his best shot, hitting Flowers in the right arm.

He heard the cries of anguish turn into yelps of pain, and Flowers began to curse. Cole could see the flashing sirens coming closer to their location, and from his position on the ground he saw Flowers's heavy boots running between the cars to make an escape. Cole sprang to his feet and immediately went to Deborah's side, pulling her hands away from her head where she had shielded herself from the noise. He watched Flowers run from the scene. There was no point in pursuing an unstable man armed with an assault rifle. He just hoped the police would pick him up without anybody else being hurt.

"It's okay," he said to Deborah. "He's gone. You're safe."

She wrapped her arms around his neck and held on tight. "Thank you," she said breathlessly. She then quickly pulled away. "Where's Dr. Cortas?"

In unison they looked over to the spot where the doctor had been standing. He was sprawled on the pavement, blood pooling beneath his white, tailored shirt.

Deborah rested her head against Cole's firm torso and allowed her tears to fall freely onto his T-shirt. He said nothing, and she was grateful for that. She was still trying to make sense of what had happened. While shielded by the car, she'd prayed so hard for the lives of Cole and the doctor. It was the only power she had, yet Dr. Cortas had been shot several times, injuring vital organs. She eyed the clock—five hours had passed since they'd arrived at the hospital, and Dr. Cortas was still in surgery. And there was no news on the whereabouts of Harold Flowers.

The door to the waiting room opened and Frank walked solemnly in, followed closely by a man and a woman with police badges clipped to their belts. The corridor seemed to be teeming with uniformed officers, and the hospital was buzzing about the shooting.

Frank sat down opposite them. "Dr. Cortas's surgery is going well," he said. "He's suffered terrible injuries, but he's fighting hard." He looked up at the two detectives in the room. "This is Detective Stephen Reeves and Detective Sharon Weaver. They have a lot of questions to ask you both."

Deborah lifted her head from Cole's chest and wiped away the tears. The news that Dr. Cortas was fighting hard lifted her spirits a little, but she had already given her story to the uniformed officers and she didn't want to go over it yet again. She wanted to go home with Cole, hold him close and leave all this behind. She put a hand over her mouth as she realized what her brain, in its tired and emotional state, was contemplating. She was imagining falling into Cole's embrace and taking comfort in the sense of security he offered. The day had obviously taken its toll, and she wasn't thinking straight.

"Frank," she said, looking him dead in the eye. "Dr. Cortas was on his way over here to confess that eight vials of his illegal drug Cyclone were stolen from his house, and some of those vials have been injected into the children in Pediatrics."

Frank held up his hands with his palms forward. "I know. The police filled me in on all the details you told them. The pediatric unit has been placed on lockdown, and all staff are being searched before entry."

"Has my team finished the security upgrades?" Cole asked.

"They're working around the clock to get them done by tomorrow morning," Frank replied. "We've expanded the upgrades to include the entire hospital. With swipe card entry systems in every department, there's no way anybody can get past our new systems."

Deborah wasn't convinced. "I hope you're right, Frank, because somebody has been deliberately trying to hurt our children and you weren't willing to listen." She knew that playing the blame game wouldn't help, but she couldn't stop herself. "All you cared about was the reputation of the hospital."

Frank looked down at the floor. "I'm so sorry, Deborah," he said quietly. "Your suspicions were correct all along, and I failed to protect my patients and staff." He lifted his eyes back to hers. "It goes without saying that your suspension has been lifted immediately and expunged from your record."

At this point Detective Sharon Weaver stepped forward. "We would advise Deborah not to return to work until we have located Harold Flowers. He seems to be convinced that Deborah is involved in drug tampering in the hospital, and we believe he may still be in the Erie area. He escaped from the scene in a stolen vehicle that was found on the shores of the lake a couple hours ago. It looks like he's bleeding from a bullet wound, so he may need medical help."

Deborah suddenly felt an icy chill, and she shivered. "Do you think he may come back for me?"

The detectives exchanged worried glances. "This man's history suggests that he doesn't give up easily," Detective Reeves said. "So, yes, we think there's a good chance he'll come back, which is why we want to post uniformed officers at your home for protection."

Deborah looked at Cole. She didn't know what she expected from him, but she needed him to take over, to step in and provide a buffer between her and the world.

Cole knew exactly how she was feeling without her finding the words. He rose from his seat to face the detectives. "Let's get the witness statements over and done with, because I intend to take Deborah home and make sure she has everything she needs to ride out this storm." He glanced down at her. "We'll make it through."

He sounded so sincere that she almost believed him.

NINE

Cole stood at the kitchen window in Deborah's house looking out to the street. Just beyond her front yard, parked at the edge of the curb, was a police car with two officers inside. The detectives believed that the highly visible officers would deter Flowers should he return to try to hurt Deborah again. Cole wasn't so sure. A man as unstable as Harold Flowers was capable of exceptionally reckless behavior, unafraid of punishment.

Cole saw Deborah's face reflected in the glass. She was standing behind him. He found it impossible to control his physical reaction to her presence in the room—his skin prickled with a mixture of excitement and anticipation, just as it had on the day he first approached her in high school and shyly asked her out on a date. He turned around, leaned on the kitchen counter, and she stood in front of him, hands on hips. She had showered and changed into yoga pants and a T-shirt, and she seemed to have calmed considerably since arriving home from the hospital.

"You want some coffee?" she asked.

He smiled. "That's just what I need right now."

She filled the coffeepot with water. "I've been thinking about what Flowers said about me helping Dr. Cortas to inject Cyclone into the kids at the hospital." She poured the water into the coffee machine and added the beans. "Somebody has filled his head with lies, obviously covering their own tracks." She switched on the machine and it whirred to life grinding the beans. "Do you think Frank could be the true culprit? As the hospital administrator, he has access to all parts of the hospital and all patients. Nobody would even question his presence in the pediatric unit."

"You said that Frank lives for the good reputation of the hospital," Cole said. "Why would he deliberately destroy it?"

Deborah put her palm on her forehead. "Oh, I just don't know. Nothing makes sense."

Cole stood close to her. She smelled of soap and freshly washed clothes. "Then don't try to make sense of it," he said. "The police are outside, Flowers is being hunted down, the pediatric unit is on lockdown, and you are in need of some peace and quiet."

Deborah kept her eyes on the coffee machine, watching the dark brown liquid drip into the pot. "Thank you, Cole," she said with a surprising degree of awkwardness. "I don't know anyone else I could turn to at a time like this. I don't want to worry my family or friends, and even if I did ask them for help, they're not military trained like you are." She finally lifted her eyes to meet his, and his heart skipped a beat. "It looks you came back to Harborcreek at just the right time."

He smiled. "It looks that way."

"Are you happy to be back?" The smile on her face seemed frozen and unnatural.

"Why?" he asked.

"I just wondered if you would be making your home here permanent."

He searched her eyes for evidence of what she wanted him to say, and he saw nothing but barriers. "What would you like me to do?" he asked. "Do you want me to stick around?"

She blinked quickly and busied herself retrieving cups from the shelf and then opening the fridge. He watched her with quiet interest. Her physical reaction told him far more than her words ever could. He began to wonder whether she truly cared if he stayed or left.

"What I want is irrelevant," she said. "It's what you want that matters."

He walked to her. She hooked her hair behind her ear and poured the coffee into the cups. Her fingers trembled slightly. He took the pot from her hand and put it on the counter. Then he grasped her shoulders and turned her around to face him.

"It matters a whole lot to me what you want," he said. "I can't imagine not having you in my life. It feels so natural to be with you."

She said nothing in reply.

"I never forgot you, Debs," he continued. "After I came back all those years ago and found out you were engaged to some other guy, I knew I'd blown my chance with you, but I never forgot you."

She looked down at her hands, clasped together above her navel. "Sometimes I wonder what my life would be like now if I'd married Brad. Would I have grown to love him? Would I be happier? Would I have a family?" She shrugged. "I guess I'll never know."

He took a step closer. She didn't push him away, so he remained there. "Do you sometimes regret not marrying him?"

She raised her head. Her lips were just inches from his. "I occasionally wonder about it, but I have no regrets. He wasn't meant to be my husband." She looked into Cole's eyes. "He wasn't you."

He didn't need to hear any more. He pressed his mouth on hers and felt the tension release from his body immediately. Her lips seemed to sink into his, and she slid her arms around his waist, closing her eyes and relaxing her shoulders. He buried his hand in her hair and rested his fingers on the back of her neck, feeling the familiar smoothness in the dip of her nape. He could scarcely believe he was holding her in his arms again after all these years. Could he really have another chance at happiness? He had sealed his heart up so tight against another relationship, but that was before he had kissed Deborah for the first time in ten years. For her, he'd unseal his heart in an instant.

She pushed against him and he released her. "You said you can't imagine not having me in your life, but I'm not totally sure of the reason why. Do you truly want me in your life, or are you just trying to make amends for hurting me?"

He didn't want to rake over old ground again. "Why do you need to analyze my reasons? Can't you just accept that I care for you?"

"No, I can't," she said, her eyes becoming hard and wide. "It's not that easy."

Cole sensed that the conversation was about to take a turn for the worse, and he tried to steer it back on course. "I needed to acknowledge that I behaved badly," he said, choosing his words carefully. "And put things right."

She put her palms on his chest and pushed. He took a step back. "Why does that make me feel like a charity case?" she said. "You came back to Harborcreek to make *yourself* feel better about the past, right?"

The situation was slipping from his grasp, and he

racked his brain for a way to make it right. The tiny moment of tenderness with Deborah had been fleeting, but had reawakened something deep inside. "No," he said strongly. "I've made plenty of mistakes in the past, and I've learned to accept them. Do I feel bad? Yes, I do, but I can't change things. I didn't come back to town to serve out a punishment. I came to try to build a future."

Her anger abated. She touched her lips. "A future with me?"

"I never ever thought I'd be so lucky to have that option," he said honestly. "I knew you'd be angry with me and be wary of my reasons for coming home."

"We can never go back to how we were, Cole," she said. "That's long gone."

"Don't you think I know that?" he said, trying not to sound irritated. "But we could have something different, something better."

She narrowed her eyes at him. The sun streaming through the window lit up her face and her blond curls seemed to cast a glow around her head. "Something better?" she questioned. "I want to get married and have a family, Cole. You said yourself that you don't want to bring another child into the world." She shook her head. "How can we possibly have something better when we want totally different things?"

Cole stood in silence. She had floored him with her argument. His experience of fatherhood had ended in disaster, and he had vowed never to return to that desolate place. She took his silence as agreement. "Can we just forget the kiss ever happened?" she asked, running her hands through her hair. "It was a mistake." She picked up her coffee cup. "I won't make the same mistake twice."

"Debs," he said, reaching out and touching her shoulder. "It may have been a mistake for you, but it felt so right to me."

"I'm going up to my bedroom," she said, ignoring his words. "I have to make some calls." She headed for the door. "Help yourself to anything you need in the kitchen."

"Please, Deborah," he implored, watching her go. "Can't we just talk about it?"

She padded up the stairs without answering. Cole clenched his hands tightly into balls and flexed his biceps. He had come so agonizingly close to winning Deborah back, but had been stopped dead in his tracks. She wanted all the things that any woman her age naturally wanted—marriage, family, stability. But she knew he couldn't provide these vital basics, and he wasn't able to reassure her that he could.

He paced the room, wondering if he had held her in his arms for the very last time.

Deborah lay on her bed in a fetal position and willed herself not to cry. She clenched her fists, digging her nails into her palms, giving her a welcome distraction of discomfort. She had remained so strong and steadfast right up until this moment. She had successfully managed to convince herself that she was over Cole, that he meant nothing to her, but it all came crashing down the minute she allowed his lips to touch hers. Now she was forced to admit that her feelings for him were not as simple as she'd tried to make them. She had gotten over the boy who had abandoned her ten years ago, but now she was falling for the man who had returned in his place.

No, she muttered to herself, *he is not the right man for you.*

Her mind was awash with images she couldn't push back—gunfire streaming through the air, the cacophony of noise, smoke billowing from crushed metal, Dr. Cortas lying in dark, sticky blood. And Cole's face appeared in the midst of the harsh, violent images, calming her mind. His face made her feel safer and more secure. Yet it also made her resentful and angry. He had waltzed back into her life and turned it upside down in a matter of days. He had reeled her in like a fish with his twinkling green eyes and wide smile, making her almost believe they could have a future together. He knew he didn't want another family, yet he had played her like a piano. The more she thought about it, the more resentful she grew. Well, this would be the last time he played her. The very last time.

She sat up and reached for her cell on the nightstand. She scrolled through her contacts and found the direct number for Pediatrics. There were many people she needed to check on.

The phone was picked up instantly.

"Hi, Diane," Deborah said, recognizing the voice on the other end. "It's me."

"Oh, Deborah!" Diane exclaimed. "How are you? I heard about the shooting incident on the highway. The police are swarming all over the hospital like ants. It's crazy."

"I'm fine," she said. "Much better than Dr. Cortas. How is he?"

"No change," Diane said. "He's in the ICU on life support. Only close family allowed, and there are two policemen standing guard outside his room." She went quiet for a moment. "Frank is walking around looking totally dazed. I don't think he can believe what's happened."

Deborah felt anxious at the mention of Frank's name. "Has Frank been in to see Dr. Cortas?" she asked.

"I think so," Diane replied. "He's working late tonight, keeping a close eye on everything and everyone. He's even having us searched before we come into the unit."

Deborah rose from her bed and walked to the window. The sun was setting and the last haze of sunshine was clinging to the air. "Does anyone search him?"

"I don't know. Why do you ask?"

"Think about it, Diane," Deborah said. "Frank is the only person who can bypass all security procedures, because he's in charge of the entire hospital."

She heard Diane give a theatrical gasp on the end of the line, as though she didn't believe what Deborah was suggesting. "You think Frank is the one who's been injecting Cyclone into the children?"

"How do you know about Cyclone?" Deborah asked.

"Frank told me the whole story," Diane said. "He said something about a girl who died in Chicago, and now the dad is out for revenge."

Deborah shook her head in exasperation. "Frank was supposed to keep it all under wraps for now," she said with irritation. "The police don't want the story leaking out to the press until the man who shot Dr. Cortas is caught." An idea hit her. "But if Frank lets the story leak out, then it would give him some drama to hide behind. The more I think about it, the more I worry that he's the one who stole the Cyclone from Dr. Cortas in order to continue the clinical trial at Harborcreek."

"You really think Frank would do that?"

"If you'd asked me that question a week ago, I'd have said no, but I'd also have said that Dr. Cortas had nothing to hide." Deborah closed her drapes. "People can surprise you. I'd never have thought Frank would do anything to damage the reputation of the hospital, but he may be working on the principle that all publicity is good publicity."

"Do you want me to watch him?" Diane said. "I've been trying to keep a close guard on the staff in Pediatrics, but it's difficult to monitor everyone. Now we have the new security cameras, it'll be harder for anyone to interfere with any patient medicines unnoticed."

Deborah checked the clock. Realizing the time, she said, "Diane, you shouldn't even be at the hospital. Your shift finished at five. It's quarter after eight."

"I wanted to stay until the children were settled in for the night. They know something big is going on, and they don't want to go to sleep."

Deborah looked at the floor and sighed. She felt so lonely and isolated shut away from the hospital, unable to help.

"Deborah," Diane said. "Are you there? Are you okay?"

"Yeah, I'm here. Go home, Diane. You have a baby growing inside you, and that's more important than anything. Don't worry about keeping an eye on Frank. Leave him to me."

"Are you sure you're okay?" Diane asked. "You sound really sad."

A soft knock echoed through the room. "I'm totally fine, Diane," she answered. "Oh, I almost forgot to ask, how is Dr. Warren?"

"She's back at work and fully recovered. She thinks the sickness was a stomach bug."

"Good," Deborah said. "At least that's one less person to worry about."

The knock came again. She said goodbye and hung up the phone before calling out, "Come in."

Cole's head appeared from behind the door. "I was going to start on dinner. I wondered if you're hungry."

She shook her head.

"Deborah, you have to eat something," he said, coming into the room. "I can bring it up on a tray." He tried to raise a smile. "Think of it as room service."

Deborah bit her lip. "Cole, I've been thinking about you staying here. With the police outside, I guess I'm pretty safe by myself." She sat on the edge of her bed and looked up at him. "You don't need to stay with me."

The thought of Cole sleeping under the same roof as her was too painful to bear. She had tried so hard to let go of the hurt he'd caused, but it still lingered in her bloodstream, coursing through her veins whenever her temper flared.

He folded his arms and crossed his ankles as he leaned against the wall. Wearing blue jeans and a tight T-shirt, he looked like a member of a boy band, but less clean-cut. "I know I don't *need* to stay here with you," he said. "But I want to."

"Well, maybe *I* don't want you to," she said, fixing him with a stare. In her head, her voice continued silently, *You won't break my heart again.*

"Is this all about me kissing you?" he asked.

"No." She cast her eyes downward.

It wasn't just about the kiss. It was about the years she had spent wondering where he was, whom he was with, whether he was missing her, whether she occupied his thoughts as much as he did hers. The kiss had brought all these memories flooding back and, worse than that, she had enjoyed feeling Cole's lips on hers again. She hated herself for reopening old wounds. And she hated Cole for working his way back into her affections.

"I'm sorry about the kiss," he said. Then he shook his

head and stood up straight. "Actually, I'm *not* sorry about the kiss, and I'd do it again a million times over, but I'm mature enough to know when to back off."

His confrontational stance sent her resentment bubbling to the surface. "Of course, we already know how easily you give up and walk away."

He threw his hands in the air. "What do you want from me, Debs?" he asked, his voice rising. "Do you want me to walk away, or do you want me to fight to win you back? Because I just don't know."

She jumped up from the bed, her hair bouncing with the force. "Why would I want you to fight for me, Cole?" she shouted. "You've never made the slightest effort to fight for me in the past, so I sure don't expect you to start now."

He faced her head-on. "Do you think I don't care?"

She gritted her teeth. "I know you don't care."

His face looked genuinely pained and for a moment Deborah regretted her words. But the moment passed quickly and she found her wrath again. He had promised to love her forever, and she had assumed he would fight tooth and nail to stay by her side. Yet he'd tossed her aside like yesterday's garbage. How could she believe that he cared for her now? How could she ever trust his sincerity? He was a liar.

"Just leave," she spat at him, remembering his long legs striding along the water's edge. "You know how to do *that*, right?"

"I know you're hurting," he said, taking a step toward her. "Anger like this only ever comes from pain."

"Oh, so now you're an expert on how I feel," she said, crossing her arms in a defensive posture. "Well, thank you for the amazing insight into my anger issues. However did I manage for ten years without you?"

He stood in front of her, sadness on his face. "I'm sorry, Debs," he said gently. "I'm sorry for abandoning you. I'm sorry for breaking all my promises to you. But, most of all, I'm sorry for not letting you vent your anger on me when you most needed to."

Something deep inside her snapped like a coiled spring that had been wound too tight for too long. She almost heard it ping inside her chest. A sob left her lips. "I hate you."

He didn't flinch. "I love you."

She pointed to the door. "Get out."

He turned and was gone in a few seconds, leaving her with only the strength to throw herself onto the bed, bury her face in a pillow and let out ten years of pain in one big, muffled howl.

Cole walked downstairs and sat on the couch. He knew Deborah was letting all her anger and frustration come out, and he also knew he couldn't help. Dillon had been right. She was testing him, pushing him to see if he would throw in the towel and leave. He hadn't meant to say the words *I love you*. In fact, he had surprised himself by admitting that he still loved Deborah. He had probably never stopped loving her. His ex-wife had once told him she thought his true affections belonged elsewhere, and it turned out she was right. Deborah had stolen his heart in high school, and she still had it. The question was—did she still want it?

He heard movement upstairs. Deborah was walking around her room, opening drawers, slamming them shut, still venting her frustration. He would gladly allow her to vent on him. After all, he was the one who truly deserved it. But he needed to let her take the lead and reach her own conclusions. She was a strong-minded woman—this much he knew.

The door to her bedroom creaked open and he heard her footsteps on the carpeted stairs. He watched her through the open door as she stood in the hallway, bringing her face close to the mirror and rubbing streaks from beneath her eyes. Then she ran her fingers through her hair, took a deep breath and joined him in the living room.

"I want to apologize," she said, holding her head high. "I should never have said that I hated you. *Hate* is such an ugly word. It was wrong of me."

"No apology necessary," he said. "I totally understand."

Her fists clenched as she spoke. "I'm really ashamed of how I let my temper get the better of me. It was only after I prayed that I calmed down and realized how unkind my words were."

He rose from his seat. "Listen," he said. "We all say things we regret in the heat of the moment. We're only human, and God knows that. I just hope that you're not going to ask me to leave again." He jerked his head over to the window. "I know the police are outside, but you saw how determined Flowers was. He's heavily armed, and if he comes looking for you, I want to be here."

She nodded.

"So I can stay?" he asked tentatively.

"Only until Flowers is caught," she said. "Then you leave immediately."

"Sure."

She looked at the floor. "Can we forget that last conversation ever happened?"

He thought of his own actions in the heat of the moment, and the words he'd spoken—*I love you*. "Don't you want to talk about what I just said?" he asked.

"No."

He didn't want to leave so many unanswered questions. "Are you sure?"

"I'm sure," she said. "I don't want to talk about us anymore. I want to find out who's responsible for injecting Cyclone into the children in Pediatrics and trying to frame me." She sat in an armchair, legs tightly pressed together, hands on knees. She looked uncomfortable. "I think we should focus on Frank Carlisle. He's my number one suspect right now, and I'm really concerned that he still has vials of the drug in his possession."

"Do you want to talk to the police about it?"

"There's no point," she said. "Frank would deny any involvement, and I have no proof. I think it would be better if I speak to him directly. Frank and I have worked together for eight years. I want to look into his eyes when I ask the question."

Cole studied her face. She was pale and tired. "We'll go to the hospital together tomorrow. Remember that you can't go anywhere without a bodyguard, so wherever you go, I go."

"It's Sunday tomorrow. Frank doesn't work on Sundays."

"You want to go right now?"

"Frank is working late tonight, so I know he'll be there." She pushed her hair behind her ears. "I hate being so far away from the children. What if something bad happens to them and nobody's there to help? It's awful not knowing whether they're safe or not."

Cole bowed his head. "That's exactly how I feel. Not being able to protect a child from harm is gut-wrenching."

"Are you talking about the kids at the hospital or those kids you buried in Afghanistan?" She dropped her voice. "Or Elliot?"

He couldn't help but smile, even though he felt joyless. She knew him well. "All of them," he said. "I don't want to fail another child."

"Is that how you feel?" she asked. "Like a failure?"

He met her eyes. "I felt like a failure as a soldier when I couldn't save those girls in Afghanistan, and I felt like a failure as a father when Elliot died."

"You don't have to be defined by your past experiences, no matter how tragic they are," she said. "What's done is done and can't be undone. You have to move forward and focus on the future instead."

He shifted on the couch to position himself closer to her chair. "That goes for both of us, you know."

She visibly shrank back in her seat, as though his words had physically pushed her. "I know. I admit that I've struggled to come to terms with you being back here in Harborcreek. The only way I could deal with our breakup was to try to hate you." She laughed in a high, brittle way. "And I really wanted to hate you, Cole. I tried my best to see you as the bad guy, but it just didn't work. You're not a bad guy—you're kind and generous and good-hearted. I can't help but like you." She wiped away a tear. "Which is way worse than hating you." She looked him squarely in the eye, and he saw deep inside for the first time since his return. "It would be so much easier if you were a jerk," she said.

He smiled. "I've only been back a little while. Give me time."

He was pleased to see her laugh.

Deborah recovered her composure and took a big calming breath, then pulled a tissue from a box on the table. "Anyway, I'm glad we cleared the air. If you're going to be living here, I don't want it to be awkward when we run into each other."

"I don't want it to be awkward, either," he said. "But I'd like to be more than somebody you say hi to in the supermarket."

She rose from her chair, adjusted the waistband of her pants. "We already discussed this, Cole. We want different things."

He rose to stand with her. "I know it's complicated, but can't we at least discuss the possibility of being more than friends?"

"This conversation is over," she said, walking to the hallway to grab a fleece jacket. "We're wasting time here when we could be checking on the children at the hospital."

He opened his mouth to speak but was distracted by a shadow running past the window.

Deborah zipped up the jacket and stood by the front door. "You wanna drive?"

As she reached for the handle, a sensation of overwhelming panic overtook him and he launched himself toward her, grabbing hold of her arms, thrusting her back. She looked shocked and confused as she fell to the floor, knocking over the hallway table and lamp on the way down.

When a hailstorm of bullets peppered the front door, she understood what Cole had already anticipated. They were under attack.

TEN

Deborah tried to scramble away from the door, but Cole held her firmly in his arms on the floor. He had positioned the hallway table directly between them and the door, giving them an extra barrier from the bullets. Splinters from the wooden door were spitting down onto the carpet, and there was no escape from the noise reverberating through the house. Deborah had a feeling this was the final showdown between them and Flowers. She somehow knew he would leave her house in one of two ways—as the victor or in a body bag.

The gunfire ceased and the door opened with one powerful kick. Cole was ready and took aim with his gun, firing rapidly at the looming figure of Mr. Flowers, still wearing his bulletproof vest, now stained dark red with blood from the bullet wound on his shoulder. The addition of a gas mask completed his war zone outfit, giving him an air of invincibility. Cole's bullets pounded into Mr. Flowers's protective vest, and his body jerked and jarred with each blow, forcing him backward. The ferocity of the defense was clearly unexpected and Mr. Flowers turned and ran, ducking low on the deck outside. The air around them began to fill with misty particles that caused Deborah's eyes and throat to burn.

"There's tear gas outside," Cole yelled, grabbing Deborah's hand and yanking her to her feet. "That's how he got past the police." He pulled her toward the stairs. "We need to get away from the smoke and find somewhere for you to hide."

In her panicked state, Deborah had trouble keeping her balance and she stumbled. Cole kept a tight hold on her, taking almost her entire body weight when yanking her up the stairs. She could hear Flowers outside, cursing and making threats. Cole's fierce, armed resistance had made him more cautious, but she reckoned they had only a matter of seconds before Flowers came looking for her.

They reached the top of the stairs and Cole spun around to face her. "Where is the best place for you to hide?" he asked. "I can hold him off while we wait for police backup."

Deborah's throat was almost too dry to speak. The acidic taste in her mouth was the only moisture on her tongue, and the tear gas had made her eyes well up with water. She pointed to the hatch leading to the attic. "Up," she managed to croak.

Cole jumped and caught the cord that hung down to open the attic entrance. The trap fell, swinging on its hinges to reveal the dark, dusty space above.

"Where's the ladder?" Cole asked anxiously, looking at the three-foot gap between them and the hole.

Deborah couldn't think for a minute. She shook her head, trying to clear the fog in her brain. Mr. Flowers was still on the porch, shouting his threats, but soon he would be inside. He would come for her.

"Um..." she said, rubbing her temples. "The ladder's broken. I use a stepladder from the garage."

"I'll lift you up," he said quickly, clutching her waist

and hoisting her onto his shoulders. "Grab the edges and pull yourself inside."

Deborah steadied herself on Cole's shoulders and reached for the edges of the hatch, gripping them with her fingertips. Using all her strength, she tried to haul her weight from Cole's shoulders using only her arms. She just didn't have the power to do it, and her grip was lost. Her body fell but, before she reached the floor, Cole caught her in his arms and put her on her feet.

"I'll have to lift you up from inside," he said, holstering his gun and jumping high into the air to clasp the rim of the entrance hole with both hands. He effortlessly pulled his body into the attic in one smooth movement.

"Cole," she called, hearing Flowers's footsteps on her porch. "Hurry. Please hurry."

Cole leaned out of the hatch and stretched his arms, fingers splayed. She put her hands into his and was lifted clean off her feet in a matter of seconds, gliding upward as if weightless. The darkness of the attic enveloped her, and the musty smell made her cough. Cole steered her to one side, leaned back down to the hatch and snatched it closed, sealing them in the darkness.

In the gloom, Deborah saw Cole raise a finger to his lips, warning her to remain still and quiet. She could hear heavy footsteps on the stairs—the slow measured pace of a man who knew his victim was cornered. The footsteps went into her bedroom, and Cole pulled her to her feet, pointing to a small ventilation unit in the roof.

He put his lips next to her ear. "I'll punch through the vent and lift you out onto the roof," he said quietly. She heard her closet door being opened and hangers being yanked from the rails. Mr. Flowers was searching for her. It was only a matter of time before he realized their hiding place was above his head.

Cole picked up an old paint-spattered cloth from the floor and wrapped it around his hand before hitting the vent a number of times, punching it hard with his protected right fist. In no time, the vent popped out onto the roof, leaving a narrow hole just big enough for her to squeeze through.

"If it's safe for you to climb down to the ground, do it," Cole continued. "Otherwise, stay on the roof until I come back for you."

"Are you staying in the house?" she whispered. Flowers had moved into her bathroom. She heard the rip of the shower curtain as it was torn from its hooks in a series of pops.

Cole was guiding her to the hole. "I need to stop this guy once and for all," he said. "I won't let him get to you."

Deborah felt herself being lifted by her hips and pushed out into the night air. She positioned herself on the sloping roof, sitting down for better stability. The sandpaper texture of the shingles snagged on her clothes, ensuring she didn't slip. The lights of Harborcreek stretched out before her and in the distance a convoy of flashing red lights lit up the streets, heading their way. Help was coming.

Cole's face was still visible in the hole through which she had just escaped. "Don't come back inside no matter what you hear, okay?"

The brisk wind was cold on her skin. "You'll come back, right?"

He smiled a wide smile. "I always do, Dee."

Then he was gone and she inched her way down the roof, heading for a downspout that might allow her to climb to the ground. She could see one of the police officers hunched on the grass in her front yard, vomiting from the effects of the tear gas. His partner was coughing uncontrollably and gasping for breath, walking blindly away from the house as if unable to see. A canister no bigger than a soda can lay on the ground, spewing the last of its toxic contents into the air, sending swirling vapors curling around the patrol car at the curb. The officers had clearly taken a big hit, and had been temporarily incapacitated. They would be of no help to Cole for a good while yet. Her neighbors were twitching drapes with anxious faces, some holding phones to their ears, reporting the devastating scene outside.

You can do this, she said to herself, rallying her defenses and edging her way down to the drainpipe. It looked sturdy, so she took a tight hold of the top and tried to twist her body around to hug the metal tube tightly. Her sneakers squeaked on the shiny surface and slipped slightly, so she adjusted her grip, holding on to the pipe like a monkey clutching its mother. In this position, she could shimmy down slowly. She tried not to think of Cole inside. She also tried not to think of the way he had said *I love you* as if it was the most natural thing in the world.

"Lord, keep Cole safe," she muttered as she reached her bedroom window. Thankfully, she had closed the drapes earlier and was hidden from view.

She looked below and saw Mr. Rafferty come running from his yard, a cloth covering his mouth. He stopped briefly to check on the officer kneeling on the ground, and then continued to her house, coming to stand directly beneath her.

He removed the cloth from his mouth. "Deborah," he called. "Jump down."

She prepared herself for the drop into the waiting

arms of her stoutly built neighbor and took a deep breath. A sudden explosion of gunfire from inside the house took her off guard, and she lost her hold. She fell quickly, the thick stems of a hydrangea bush digging hard into her back. She shouted out in pain and rolled onto the grass, landing at the feet of a terrified-looking Mr. Rafferty.

Cole opened the hatch a tiny crack and observed the movements below. He watched Flowers walk from room to room, his face darkening in anger and confusion at being unable to locate Deborah or Cole. The deranged man clearly didn't have the presence of mind to consider an attic. Finally, he snapped and vented his temper, spraying the wall in the hallway with bullets in his frustration. Cole knew that his gun would be of little use in taking this man down safely. Any shot he took would only have the power to wound a part of the body not protected by specialist clothing—maybe an arm or leg. That wouldn't be enough to stop Flowers from shooting back. The only other option was to take a head shot, and that seemed an unfair punishment on a man who wasn't in his right mind. Cole needed an alternate plan. As the bullets peppered the wall, opening up ragged holes, he flipped open the hatch, steadied himself in a crouching position on the ledge and launched himself into the air.

He landed on Flowers's back and wrapped his arms around the big man's torso. The assault rifle went wildly out of control as the two men grappled, sending bullets in every direction. Cole grabbed the barrel of the gun, knowing it would be hot, and grimaced against the searing pain in his hand. The firing stopped and Cole yanked the barrel forward, smacking it hard into Flowers's gas mask. It was enough to daze Flowers and he staggered on his feet.

Cole worked his fingers beneath the gas mask and wrenched it off, exposing his assailant's face and head. Then he jerked the barrel of the gun toward the exposed face, using all the power he could muster. He heard a crack and a cry of agony as blood rushed down Flowers's face. The older man brought his hands to his nose, giving Cole the perfect opportunity to yank the strap of the AK-47 from Flowers's shoulder and hurl the weapon toward the stairs. The gun bounced off the handrail before falling over the edge and clattering to the bottom.

"Now," Cole said, tensing his arm around Flowers's neck and putting him in a choke hold. "This contest just got a whole lot fairer."

Flowers began to make gurgling noises and Cole loosened his grip. He didn't want to kill an unarmed man, no matter how vile his actions. Instead, he tried to yank Flowers's arms around his back to put him in a position of restraint. But it only allowed him to recover a little and find renewed strength, pushing against Cole so hard that he slammed into the wall. Both men were coughing from the tear gas. Cole made a grab for his holstered gun. So did his assailant, and they both had their hands on the weapon, pitted against each other in a test of power.

Flowers clearly felt the younger, fitter man gaining the upper hand and lunged toward Cole's face, baring his teeth, trying to bite his cheek. Cole turned away and, in the next moment, felt the gun discharge a bullet from the chamber. Flowers's body gave a sudden and violent jerk. Cole felt warm blood cascade over his hand, and he saw with horror that a gaping wound had opened up on Flowers's neck, pumping out blood faster than a spring of water.

The injured man went down to his knees, pressing his

neck with the palm of his hand. Cole tried to stem the flow of blood with his own hand, but both men knew it was futile. The jugular vein had been hit, and his fate was already sealed.

Flowers batted away Cole's hand with the last of his strength, looked him in the eye with a calm smile and said, "I'm ready." They were his last words before he fell to the floor.

Cole sat by Mr. Flowers, holding his clammy hand as his face turned white and his lips blue, feeling an overwhelming sensation of anger and sadness that this man had dealt with his daughter's death this way. The tears that streamed down Cole's face were partly due to the tear gas, but also in recognition of the pointless waste of life he had just witnessed. This father's grief had destroyed him. As he heard the wail of police sirens grow louder, Cole realized the same thing had almost happened to him. He had made the mistake of allowing his grief to govern his future. Just like Flowers, he had given up on the chance of being happy again after losing his precious child.

But God had seen Cole's pain, and God had brought him home.

Deborah and her neighbor settled the two coughing officers on the porch steps of Mr. Rafferty's house and poured milk into their red-rimmed eyes. Deborah knew the soothing properties of milk were an excellent remedy for the damaging effects of the burning gas, and her neighbor had doused the smoldering canister with a hose to prevent any more toxic fumes from escaping. The sound of gunfire had ceased inside Deborah's house. There was no noise at all to give her an indication of the situation inside.

As much as she wanted to go to Cole's aid, she kept her promise to stay outside until he came for her.

Deborah felt a huge surge of relief and gratitude when several police cars screeched to a halt alongside her home. Officers in full SWAT gear jumped from the cars, guns raised.

"There's a man inside with an AK-47," she said, pointing to the house. "But there's an innocent man in there, too. Please be careful who you shoot."

"We're trained professionals, ma'am," the officer said, taking her arm and pulling her to her feet. "I suggest you move farther away for your own safety."

Deborah looked back at her home, its neat and tidy yard showing no signs of the danger inside. Was Cole lying in there, too injured to move? Or worse? The agony of not knowing caused her belly to ache.

Then almost as if she had willed it to happen, Cole appeared at the door with his hands in the air. His fingers were red with blood and his jeans were streaked and splattered with dark stains.

"Don't shoot," he called, taking small steps onto the porch. "Harold Flowers has been fatally shot. You'll find him at the top of the stairs."

The police officer reacted instinctively, aiming his gun at Cole. Several of his colleagues followed suit.

"No," Deborah cried out. "His name is Cole Strachan. He's a navy SEAL." She looked at him, standing strong and tall, arms aloft. "He's been taking care of me."

Then the familiar faces of the two detectives from the hospital appeared at her side. "We'll take care of things from here, Deborah," Detective Weaver said. "Mr. Rafferty has offered his home for you and Cole to be interviewed, so go inside while we secure the scene."

Deborah let out a long breath and started running to

Cole. He held out his arms and she jumped into them, wrapping her arms around his neck. She buried her face in his neck and closed her eyes, breathing in his scent, thankful that God had kept him safe.

"I was so scared," she whispered.

Police officers began to file past them, going into the house with weapons raised, taking no chances.

"Move away," a uniformed officer ordered and pointed to her neighbor's house.

Cole pulled Deborah away from him, took her hand in his and walked across the front yard, heading for Mr. Rafferty's home. Mrs. Rafferty was standing on her porch, drawing her cardigan tightly across her chest, anxiously watching her husband speak to a police officer a couple feet away.

Mrs. Rafferty placed her hand on Deborah's shoulder. "Are you okay, sweetie?" she asked. "What an awful thing to happen. What a blessing your boyfriend was there to look after you, huh?"

Deborah didn't bother to correct her neighbor's mistake. She simply nodded.

Cole led her a couple steps away. He held her face in his hands. "Harold Flowers can't hurt you now."

Deborah felt a mixture of emotions. She felt relief but also sorrow that a grief-stricken man had lost his life. "Thank you," she said.

He smiled. She sensed there was something else he wanted to say but couldn't find the words. His face was pensive and troubled.

"You did what you had to do, Cole," she said. "It was either you or him."

"It's not that," he replied. "Flowers gave me a wake-up call. He made me realize how destructive grief can be if you don't let it go." He glanced back at the house. "Harold

Flowers and I shared a bond—we both grieved for children we lost. He let his grief take him down the wrong path, and I won't let my grief do the same."

"What exactly are you saying, Cole?"

"I'm not totally sure," he replied, placing his hand across his heart. "But I feel a sense of peace here. It's like God has lifted a burden from my shoulders and I'm free to be happy again. When I was broken, He brought me back to Harborcreek to fix me. He brought me back to *you*."

Deborah noticed Detective Reeves come out of her house and head their way, talking animatedly on his cell phone.

"I'm glad that you feel a burden has been lifted," she said. "But I very much doubt that God brought you back to Harborcreek to build a future with me."

Cole nodded, as if he had expected that reaction. "I think that's exactly what He did. I feel reconnected to you, Deborah, like we're a team again."

"We're good together, I admit that, but God knows how much I want a family. He wouldn't ask me to give up on that dream." She crossed her arms. "Not even for you."

Detective Reeves stepped onto the porch and looked between them. "Harold Flowers has been declared dead at the scene," he said. "And the officers are both recovering from the tear gas." He pulled a notepad from his pocket. "We need to take some details from you. Your neighbor has kindly allowed the use of his home to talk."

"Of course," Deborah replied. "Shall we go inside?"

The detective opened the door and waited for Deborah to go first. She brushed past Cole and entered the hallway, trying to put his words out of her mind. She agreed with him that their connection had been rekindled, and she was dangerously close to falling crazy in love with him all over again. But what was the point in pursuing it? It could only lead to one thing: heartache.

Cole could give her love, support, laughter and his devoted protection. But without a baby, he could never give her the true happiness she craved. As much as the truth hurt, she had to accept that he wasn't her one true love.

Cole washed the blood from his hands before taking a seat next to Deborah on the sofa. She was quiet and still, staring into space as if locked away in her own thoughts.

Detective Reeves sat opposite them. "I'm sorry, Deborah," he said solemnly. "We never anticipated Harold Flowers using tear gas to bypass the officers guarding your home. We allowed you to be placed in danger and, on behalf of the police force of Harborcreek, I apologize."

"Those officers did everything they could to try to protect me," she replied. "They don't need to apologize for anything." She looked at Cole but didn't meet his eyes. "Besides, I had a personal bodyguard inside."

"Yes, you did," the detective said. "And it looks like he did a stand-up job." He turned his face to Cole. "Mr. Strachan, I need your gun for forensic analysis. Once we've run our ballistics checks, we'll return it."

Cole popped the clasp on his holster and took out his weapon, laying it on the table in front of him. Detective Reeves picked it up and placed it in a plastic bag, securing it with a zippered lock at the top.

"Will Cole face charges?" Deborah asked.

"I very much doubt it," the detective replied. "Mr. Flowers had clearly entered your home with the intent to kill you. We found a notebook in his pocket detailing how he wanted to make you suffer."

Deborah gasped. Cole shifted closer to her side. "What did it say?" she asked.

The detective waved a hand in the air. "You don't want to know the details, but he clearly held a personal grudge against you and Dr. Cortas, and strongly believed you were both harming children in your care. The words *child killer* were frequently used, and his notebook was full of references to the drug Cyclone."

"Harold Flowers blamed Dr. Cortas for the death of his daughter during the clinical trial," Cole said. "Yet he seemed much more determined to make Deborah suffer than the doctor. It doesn't seem fair."

"Actually," the detective replied with a grave tone, "Mr. Flowers had something far worse in mind for Dr. Cortas than the barrel of a gun. Police officers in Erie today searched a storage unit registered to Mr. Flowers and found a considerable amount of torture equipment inside."

"Torture equipment!" Deborah exclaimed. "Really?"

"I'm afraid so. There was also enough food and water for several months, as well as medical supplies, so we believe that Mr. Flowers was in the process of creating some sort of torture chamber. It doesn't bear thinking about." He raised his eyebrows. "Ironically, the doctor was fortunate to have been shot by Mr. Flowers before this terrifying plan could be put into effect. He had a narrow escape."

Cole let out a long, slow breath of relief. "We've all had narrow escapes from this guy."

"What about the person responsible for injecting Cyclone into the children at the hospital?" Deborah asked. "We still don't know who's behind this."

"There's an investigation under way already, and we hope to find some answers soon." The detective's cell phone began to buzz in his pocket and he pulled it out, looked at the display. "I gotta take this. Please excuse me."

Detective Reeves rose from his seat and walked to the front porch to take the call. Cole noticed Deborah tense up and she looked straight ahead, with her hands rested flat on her knees. The skin on the knuckles of one of her hands was scraped off, and it looked red and raw.

He reached for her hand. "You hurt yourself."

"It's nothing," she said flatly as he inspected the damaged skin. "I'll live."

"Let me at least dress it for you," he said. "I'm sure the Raffertys have a first-aid kit."

She pulled her hand away. "I said it's fine."

She sat staring at the door, giving none of her emotions away. He knew it was selfish of him to declare his love for her knowing he couldn't provide her with the most important thing she wanted in life. But he also felt himself softening, becoming open again to the point where he could maybe, just maybe, change his mind. Yet the responsibility of bringing a child into the world was so very great, and he found himself unable to take that final step. The pain of Elliot's passing was still fresh and raw. How could he ever get past that?

"That injury reminds me of the time you got your hand caught on the fence around the sport track at school," he said, retreating to the happiness of high school to give them a safe subject to talk about. "You cut it really bad, if I remember right."

She took a second or two to recall the memory. "I was holding on to the fence watching you try out for the track team," she said. "And I didn't notice that one of the metal chain links was jagged and broken. I wore a bandage for a whole week." She looked down at her fingers. "If you look close, you can still see the scar."

"But at least I made the team," he joked.

He saw her trying not to smile. "You made every team."

"Not every team," he said. "I wasn't invited to join the cheerleading squad."

A laugh escaped her lips, and he sensed her relaxing. "It's pretty hard to be a cheerleader *and* the football quarterback," she said. "Besides which, you were enemy number one with the cheerleaders after you put the mouse in the locker room."

They both laughed. After the dramatic events of the day, Cole thought it was just the therapy they needed to remind themselves that the world wasn't full of darkness.

"They were good times, huh, Debs?" he said.

She nodded. "But we can't get them back."

He took her hand, careful not to hurt her knuckles. "I'm not asking to go back. I want to go forward. I know we've been apart for ten years, and we've both changed, but the amazing bond we had is still there." He reached over to her chin and tilted her face toward him. "I know you feel it, too."

Her eyes darted between his. She looked worn-out and weary, yet beautiful.

"Do you want to know how I feel?" she asked with a sigh. "I feel scared and tired and unsure of anything. I can't deny that my belly does a flip whenever you come into the room, but that doesn't mean you're the only man who will ever make me feel that way. You're not the only man in the world, you know."

"Has any other man made your belly flip?" he asked. "Honestly?"

Her silence said it all.

"No other woman makes me feel like I can't breathe," he said. "I've been on missions to some of the most deadly places in the world and come back without a scratch, but one look at you and I'm gasping for air." He reached up and took one of her curls, twirling it around his finger. "You are my weak spot."

He noticed moisture collecting in her eyes. "I loved you with every fiber in my body, Cole. I had a vision in my head of our beautiful home, with a big backyard and a dog running around chasing a stick. I imagined us having picnics by the lake and cookouts with the neighbors. I knew it wouldn't be easy being married to a military man, but you were my hero, and I would've walked over mountains to be with you." She looked at him with an expression of such honesty and openness that he knew he was hearing the words she'd kept locked away for years. "And in the middle of this vision of our future, do you know what took center stage?"

He knew. "Children."

"Yes, children." She took his hand in hers, and her fingers were deliciously warm on his cold skin. "I can't compromise. Not after everything that's happened."

Cole looked down at their fingers twined together. He was on the verge of losing Deborah all over again. "If it means that much to you, then I'd be prepared to father a child," he said, instantly realizing that his words lacked positive impact and persuasive power. "I'd rather give you a baby than lose you again."

She withdrew her hand and shook her head sadly. "I don't want you to become a reluctant father just to keep me happy. It's not fair to me, you or a child. There's no way around this problem. I'm sorry."

He was lost for words. "But I love you, Deborah."

"Sometimes love isn't enough."

For a few seconds neither of them said a word, both knowing that they had reached an impasse. Cole had to accept defeat.

Detective Reeves came back through the door, his face showing much more strain than when he had left the room.

"That was my colleague who's leading the Cyclone investigation at Harborcreek Community Hospital," he said, retaking his seat. "It's bad news, I'm afraid."

Deborah put a palm across her forehead. "Has another child fallen ill?"

"Yes. A nine-year-old girl was given a dose of Cyclone this evening and it's caused her to go into critical renal failure. We don't yet know if she'll survive. Neither do we know how the culprit managed to bypass security."

Cole exchanged glances with Deborah, both silently acknowledging that despite the death of Harold Flowers, this dangerous situation was far from over. They would have to put their conflicting emotions aside in order to focus on those young patients who needed help. "There's one man who's capable of getting past security," she said. "Frank Carlisle."

The detective looked surprised. "The hospital administrator?"

Deborah nodded. "Outwardly, Frank seems to be doing all he can to make the hospital a safe place, but he's been very slow to act on allegations of wrongdoing."

"Actually," Cole said, "the more I think about it, the more I think Deborah's right. Frank was very reluctant to involve the police, and he delayed an investigation time and time again."

The detective settled back in his seat. "Okay. Let's talk. I want to hear the whole story."

ELEVEN

Deborah sat down in the pediatrics break room. It was Sunday morning and she should have been getting ready for church, but this matter was more important even than church. She'd wanted to rush to the hospital the previous evening, but Detective Reeves had insisted she wait.

She'd been allowed back inside her home for only a few minutes to collect some clothes and toiletries before going to her parents' house for the night. Her mother and father had been shocked to see Cole carry their daughter's bag inside their home, and she'd been forced to explain the situation. They had been horrified and dismayed, but they had thanked Cole for taking care of Deborah and invited him inside for supper. Thankfully, he'd picked up on Deborah's vibes and had made his excuses.

Now he sat by her side, clean shaven and handsome, dressed in a plain back shirt and jeans. He rested his hands on the table in front of him, cuffs rolled up to reveal a large silver watch on his left wrist. It was 8:00 a.m., and the pediatric unit was full with every staff member to be interviewed by the police. The corridors were buzzing with anxiety and disbelief. A child's life hung in the balance. And one of their team was responsible.

Deborah looked at the faces around the table—Frank, Cole, Dr. Warren and Diane. Diane sat back, rubbing her belly with both hands.

"Frank," Deborah said with a sharp tone. "How could this happen?"

Frank shook his head, cradling a cup of coffee in his hands. "I don't know. I was here myself last night, and I didn't see anything suspicious. Every member of staff is searched before entry." He bowed his head over his cup. "It's a mystery."

"Are *you* searched before entering the pediatric unit?" Deborah asked.

"Me?" Frank asked incredulously. "No, I'm not searched, but why would that be necessary?" His facial expression changed as he realized what Deborah was insinuating. "Ah, you think *I* may be the culprit."

She decided to come right out with it. "Are you?"

His response was immediate and forceful. "No."

Dr. Warren entered the conversation. She looked pale and gaunt, obviously suffering the aftereffects of her illness. "I think what Deborah is suggesting is that we should be distrustful of everybody." She pushed up her glasses. "Nobody is above suspicion, no matter how well we think we know them."

Deborah looked between Dr. Warren and Diane. "You two were here last night, right? Did you see anything unusual, maybe somebody acting odd?"

Both women shook their heads.

"My team finished up their work this morning and they installed new cameras in every corridor across the entire hospital," Cole said to Frank. "We can check the footage to see who entered this child's room. If it's not you, Mr. Carlisle, then you have nothing to fear."

"We already checked the cameras," Frank said. "But

we can't establish the identity of the culprit. This person carried a privacy screen in order to conceal their face and body." He rose from his chair and walked to the corner of the room where a lightweight fabric screen was folded. He unfolded it like a concertina and held it close to his body as he walked. "Something like this," he said from behind the screen. "All the camera picked up was a walking wall and a pair of shoes."

"What about the ID machines?" Cole asked. "That should give us a list of people who gained access to Pediatrics."

"It does," Frank said, sitting back down. "But that still leaves us with over thirty possible suspects."

Deborah kept her eyes on Frank as he spoke, watching his gestures closely. He made plenty of eye contact, his voice was level and smooth, and he didn't fidget or show anxiety. All of these signs would indicate he was telling the truth about not being involved in the crime. But Dr. Warren's words had struck a chord—nobody should be above suspicion. It was a terrifying thought.

Tears began to flow down Diane's face. "I just can't believe it," she said, covering her face with one hand and keeping the other on her belly. "That poor girl might die." A look of discomfort swept over her face and she gripped the edge of the table, grimacing.

"Are you okay, Diane?" Deborah asked, jumping up to go to her friend's side.

"I'm fine," she replied with an unnatural smile. "Just a twinge."

Dr. Warren took Diane by the hand. "Why don't I go check you over with an ultrasound," she said with a soft and reassuring tone. "It won't do any harm to take a peek."

Diane pressed her palms flat on the seat and pushed

herself up, belly forward. "Thanks, Doctor," she said, taking Dr. Warren's arm for support. "That's really kind of you."

After they left the room, Deborah took the seat Diane had vacated. It put her opposite Cole—a position she much preferred. She found it harder and harder to be in the same room as him. She had made her final decision. He did not want to be a father, and she couldn't allow him to sacrifice that firmly held desire for her sake. The only realistic choice was to put him out of her life. She met Cole's eyes with a firm stare. His tousled hair glinted under the room's strip lighting and his green eyes were intense beneath his heavy lids. He looked every inch her handsome hero, but the missing piece of the picture prevented her falling into his arms and completing the happy-ever-after.

"There's something else that I need to share with you," Frank said. "It's not yet public knowledge, but the police are interviewing a lab technician who has admitted falsifying blood test reports on the six children who suffered kidney failure."

"So that's how the toxicology reports came back clean," Deborah exclaimed. "Why did he do it?"

Frank raised his eyebrows high. "Why do most people do bad things?" he said. "For money, of course."

"Someone bribed him?" Cole asked.

"Yes," Frank answered. "And we're talking a lot of money here—hundreds of thousands of dollars."

"You're kidding," Deborah gasped. "I don't think anybody working here has access to that kind of money. Not even you, Frank."

"I guess whoever bribed the lab technician thought that money could buy his silence," Frank said. "And to some extent, it has. This guy is refusing to give a name to the police. He's lawyered up."

"But the net is closing in," Cole said. "Our bad guy won't be able to hide for long, and I think he knows it."

"The question I want answered," Deborah said, "is why somebody would do this."

Cole leaned back in his chair and put his hands behind his head. "Only one person can answer that question, and I'd very much like to be here when he's unmasked."

"I think the police have got that covered," Deborah said. "Now that your team has completed the security upgrades to the hospital, I don't think your presence is needed here any longer." She turned to the hospital administrator. "Isn't that right, Frank?"

"Well, the security work *has* been completed," Frank replied, looking over at Cole. "And I must say your team did an excellent job, Mr. Strachan. So please don't let us keep you from your other commitments. Deborah is right—you can leave anytime you wish."

Cole slid his eyes from Frank to Deborah. "I'd like to stay," he said. "Just to make sure there are no problems with the new cameras."

"There's no need," Deborah said. "We can call if anything goes wrong."

"All the same," Cole replied, leaning on his elbows across the table and enunciating his words clearly. "I'd like to stay."

Frank sensed the change in atmosphere and rose from his chair. "I can see that this is a personal issue between the two of you. I'll leave you to it."

As soon as Frank left the room, Deborah faced Cole with a hammering heart.

"I think it's time you left," she said, keeping a steely

nerve. "Now that Flowers is gone, I think I'm out of danger."

"There's an attempted murderer still on the loose," he replied. "And we have no idea who it is."

Deborah was ready. "With all the extra security at the hospital, nothing can possibly happen to me here. And if I feel threatened, I know the police will assign protection again." She smiled, but it was forced. "I'll be fine."

Cole said nothing for a while. His eyes ran all over her face, seemingly assessing her mood, formulating his response. "I'd prefer to stay."

She folded her arms. "I want you to leave."

"Why?"

"Because I do."

He tilted his head. "That's the best answer you can come up with?"

"I can't be around you anymore." Her voice was almost a whisper. "It's time we accepted that we have a fundamental difference too serious to ignore. You protect me and care for me like a husband should, but you'll never be my husband, and carrying around that knowledge is breaking my heart." She pinched her lips together, clearly trying to prevent her sadness from bursting out. "Please go. It's better for both of us to be apart."

"Can't we make one last attempt to work this out?" he asked. "I can't walk away from a love as perfect as ours without putting up more of a fight. There must be a way through."

She rose from her chair and walked into the small kitchenette to fill a glass of water. "We'd just be delaying the inevitable. I'm done talking."

She heard Cole's chair scrape on the floor. "I love you

so much, Deborah. I wish I was different. I wish I was the man you want me to be."

She felt a lump rise in her throat. "No amount of wishing will change the facts," she said with a tight voice. "You can't help how you feel. If you agreed to settle down and have kids, you'd simply be pretending to be the man I want you to be." She took a sip of water, forced the liquid down her constricted throat.

"I'd be great dad," he said. "I can promise you that."

"But don't you see, Cole, I'd always be wondering if you truly wanted to be a dad or if you were going through the motions." She put down her glass. "There really is nothing more to say."

"Can I call you later?" he asked. "To check that you're okay."

"I don't think that's a good idea," she replied. "A clean break is best."

He lingered in the doorway for a few seconds before turning, bowing his head and walking away, leaving behind a hollowness that threatened to swallow Deborah whole. She poured the water from her glass into the sink and leaned against the counter with both hands. Sending Cole away was the hardest thing she'd ever had to do, and she knew with certainty that she would never fully recover. Cole was her first love and her only love. She didn't know why God had sent him back into her life only to have him leave again so painfully, but she trusted that she was treading the path laid down for her.

And that path, much to her despair, seemed to stretch into a long, lonely distance.

Cole trudged through the parking lot outside the hospital. His legs were heavy, but not as heavy as his heart. Even though he had been prepared to give Deborah all that she wanted, it wasn't enough. He kicked at a stone on the ground and sent it skipping along the asphalt. He turned and looked up at the hospital, trying to work out which of the rows of identical windows were those of the pediatric unit. He wondered if Deborah would be standing watching him leave. Would she be feeling anywhere near the level of pain he was feeling right now?

Two police officers walked past him toward the entrance doors, going to join the many other cops already inside the hospital. The corridors were full of uniformed officers conducting interviews, taking statements, trying to narrow down the list of suspects. No way would Deborah come to harm with such a heavy police presence. And her parents would provide her with a supportive home where she could stay until hers was repaired. At least he was comforted by that knowledge.

Cole approached the Oldsmobile Dillon had given him in Pittsburgh and unlocked it. He remembered his friend's words: *You might suffer tragedies, or you might be given blessings, but you can be sure of one thing—if you don't take a chance, you'll never find out.* He wanted to take a chance on becoming a father again, but Deborah saw through his reluctance. She deserved his whole commitment, not part of it.

Cole started the car and drove through the lot, joining the highway back to his office. He could throw himself into work. He could still make a life for himself back in his hometown, even if it didn't include Deborah. He knew he was strong and resilient and could dig deep when he needed to.

His cell began to buzz in his pocket and he pulled it out. It was Deborah. He slid the handset into the holder on the dash and pressed the speakerphone button.

"Hey, Debs," he said with false cheerfulness. "Couldn't

stand to be away from me for more than five minutes, huh?"

He had to strain to hear her small voice. "After you left, I realized there was something I forgot to say."

His chest tightened. Had she changed her mind? "What?"

"I forgot to say how proud I am of the man you've become," she said. "And you shouldn't feel ashamed about the past. It's all forgotten."

He was momentarily silenced. "Wow," he said finally. "Thank you, Deborah, but what prompted this?"

"I just didn't want you to leave without knowing that the slate is wiped clean. You've proven yourself to be decent and trustworthy, and I hope you'll find happiness with somebody else."

He knew the truth. He would never find happiness anywhere unless Deborah were there. He pulled to the shoulder of the road and put the phone to his ear. "How are things at the hospital?" he asked. "Any updates?"

She went quiet.

"Deborah," he said, more firmly. "Did something happen?"

"Well, I'm not sure. It may be nothing."

He sensed she wanted to ask for his advice but didn't feel entitled, especially after sending him away. "Tell me."

"I just went to change the IV drip on one of the children, and she was holding a teddy bear just like the one left on my doorstep."

"Are you sure it was the same?"

"It was the exact same manufacturer," she said. "I checked the label. It was identical in every way."

Cole drew himself up. "Did you ask her where she got it from?"

"Yes, I did. She told me Nurse White gave it to her."

He wasn't familiar with the name. "Nurse White?"

"Diane."

"Have you asked Diane about it?"

"Not yet," she replied. "I haven't had the chance."

He smiled. He figured that Deborah wanted to run it by him first and had phoned under a false pretext. "I'm turning around and coming back to the hospital."

"No," she protested. "There's no need to do that. It's probably just a coincidence."

He ignored her protest. "I can be there in ten minutes."

"No," she repeated. "Please don't, Cole. We agreed on this."

"Okay." He'd already made up his mind, but he didn't want to waste time arguing. "If you're sure you can handle it alone, I'll stay away."

With that he disconnected and pulled a sharp U-turn to make the short journey back to the large, white building shimmering in the morning sun. Deborah had told him not to return, but his instinct told him otherwise.

It turned out that his job protecting Deborah wasn't quite over, and he needed to stay by her side for a little while longer.

Deborah washed her face and dried her tears, taking some deep breaths and giving herself a pep talk before she went to find Diane. She looked at her reflection in the mirror and groaned. Her eyes were red rimmed and puffy, made more noticeable by the contrast of her washed-out skin. She pulled mascara from her purse and applied a black coating to her lashes, standing back and blinking to assess the difference it made.

"Making yourself look pretty, huh, Deborah?"

She spun around to see Diane enter the bathroom, looking as tired and pale as she was.

Deborah slipped her mascara back into her purse, feeling embarrassed that Diane had caught her putting on makeup at such a serious time. "How are you feeling, Diane?" she asked, rubbing her friend's arm. "Would it be okay if we went somewhere and had a chat?"

"I'm okay. Dr. Warren checked me over and the baby's doing fine." Diane smiled nervously. "But I don't have time to talk right now. I've lost something, and I wonder if you could help me find it."

Deborah snapped her purse closed. Was Diane being deliberately evasive? "What did you lose?" she asked.

"It's a urine sample," Diane said. "I left it in the refrigerator in the clinical storeroom, but it's gone."

"Urine samples aren't usually stored in that fridge. You know that, Diane," Deborah replied. "Maybe it's accidentally been disposed of. Can you get another one?"

Diane wrung her hands. "No, I can't get another one, and this sample is really important. I need to find it."

Deborah heard the anxiety in Diane's voice. "Okay," she said. "Who's the patient?"

Diane didn't answer.

"What's so important about this particular sample anyway?" Deborah asked.

Diane looked uncomfortable. "I'd rather not say."

Deborah began to feel concerned. Why would Diane be secretive about something as harmless as a urine sample? "Was the specimen jar labeled?" she asked. "It surely had the patient's name on it, right?"

Diane shook her head.

"Diane," Deborah said slowly. "I can't help you if you don't give me more information. Why can't you tell me the details?"

Diane looked behind her shoulder as the door of the bathroom opened and another nurse entered. "It doesn't matter," she said with a flustered voice. "I'm sure I'll find it." She rushed from the room.

"Wait up!" Deborah called after her. "I wanted to ask you something." But Diane was heading off down the corridor as fast as a woman in her condition could walk. Deborah began to follow, determined to find out if the teddy bear was a vital clue in this investigation or nothing more than a coincidence. But she almost collided with Dr. Warren as she stepped into the hallway and was forced to stop in her tracks.

"Ah, Deborah," Dr. Warren said. "Frank sent me to find you. The police are interviewing everybody in alphabetical order. They're currently up to the letter *J*, so you'll be called in soon."

Deborah looked at Diane as she hurried around a corner. "Dr. Warren," she said. "Did you recently see Diane give a teddy bear to a little girl in room nine?"

"Yes, I did," Dr. Warren replied. "She gave out a carton of them last week. Every child got one as far as I'm aware."

"She had a whole carton?" Deborah questioned. "Where did she get them?"

"Frank wanted to do something to comfort the children after the kidney failures, so he bought them all teddy bears." She raised one eyebrow. "And with his own money. Who'd have thought he could be so generous?"

"Frank bought them?" Deborah asked. That could mean Frank gave one of those bears to Flowers to mutilate and leave on her doorstep. She put her hand to her head, uncertain who to trust. The only person she knew she could trust unfailingly and unendingly was Cole. She missed his strong, steadying influence already.

"Are you all right, Deborah?" Dr. Warren asked, taking her arm and leading her to one of the small plastic chairs lining the hallway. "You've gone as white as a sheet."

Deborah didn't want to implicate Diane or Frank before being sure of her facts. "It's complicated, but I think I should keep an eye on Diane. Her behavior is a little strange."

"I noticed that she looked very tense a moment ago," Dr. Warren said, looking down the hallway. "Where was she rushing off to in such a hurry?"

"She's looking for a urine sample that's disappeared from the refrigerator in the storeroom, but she won't tell me who it's from, or why it was there. She's being very mysterious about it."

A look of recognition passed over Dr. Warren's face. "Oh, yes, I remember seeing the sample," she replied. "It was in the fridge for over two weeks, so I moved it to the clinical waste unit. It wasn't labeled as a pediatric sample, and I assumed that Dr. Cortas was keeping it separate from the others for some reason."

"I don't know why Diane was so cagey about this particular sample," Deborah said. "Did you notice anything unusual about it?"

"Actually, I did," Dr. Warren replied. "Each time I saw it, it seemed to be getting smaller and smaller, which I thought was odd." She dropped her voice. "According to my medical experience, urine doesn't just dissolve away on its own."

"No, it doesn't," Deborah said. "I'm worried Diane is hiding something."

Dr. Warren looked grave. "Something to do with the Cyclone scandal?"

"Perhaps," Deborah said. "She could be trying to

protect somebody. Or she could be directly involved. I
need to ask her some questions."

Dr. Warren put her hand on Deborah's arm. "I'm
afraid I'm going to have to ask you to delay speaking
with her until I've had the chance to deliver some news
about her ultrasound."

"Oh, no," Deborah exclaimed. "Is there a problem?"

"I can't discuss that with you, Deborah. You know
that," Dr. Warren said. "I'll go find her right away. Stay
here until your name is called by the detectives in the
conference room. Everything else can wait."

As Deborah watched Dr. Warren stride off down the
corridor, she wrung her hands together in her lap, feeling anxious without Cole's calming voice to soothe her
whirling mind. She couldn't sit and do nothing while
there were leads to investigate.

She rose from her seat. If the answers wouldn't come
to her, then she would seek them out.

Cole parked the car and headed quickly inside. Deborah's voice on the phone had betrayed her anxiety. He
never should have left.

As he walked briskly toward the entrance doors, he
noticed Dr. Warren come out into the cool morning air.
She pulled her white doctor's coat around her slender
frame, looking in both directions.

"Hi, Dr. Warren," he called. "You looking for somebody?"

"Actually, yes," she replied. "Have you seen Diane?"

Cole shook his head. "Sorry, no, but I only just got
here. I came to make sure Deborah stays safe during
the investigation."

"I left her in Pediatrics waiting to be called into the
investigation room," Dr. Warren said. As she spoke, she

seemed distracted, her eyes flitting back and forth across the lot.

"Dr. Warren," he said, touching her arm. "Is everything all right? You seem on edge."

"Um…no, everything is not all right." The doctor was obviously loath to speak freely. "I may have some information about the Cyclone investigation, but I'm unable to talk about it because of patient confidentiality."

Cole nodded solemnly. "I understand that it's important to respect patient privacy," he said, gently guiding her back into the foyer of the hospital and then to a quiet corner. "But if you have information that may be of interest to the police, you have a duty to share it. A child's life may depend on it."

Dr. Warren gave a sigh. "Yes, you're right. But what if it turns out to just be a strange coincidence?"

Cole's senses jumped to attention. "In my experience, Doctor, there are no such things as strange coincidences. If two things appear to be connected to each other, they usually are."

Dr. Warren took a step closer to him and spoke in a whisper. "While I was checking Diane with the ultrasound machine, I noticed that the baby had an echogenic bowel."

"I have no idea what that means," Cole said. "Can you make it simple for me?"

"It's when the bowel shows up as a white spot, when it's supposed to be dark," Dr. Warren explained. "It can be a sign that something is wrong. I didn't point it out to Diane at the time, because she was distressed about the latest Cyclone incident, but her baby could have a serious condition."

Cole began to see where this might be going. "What kind of condition?"

Dr. Warren looked him straight in the eye. "The most likely one is cystic fibrosis."

All the missing pieces of the puzzle began to slot into place. "The same condition that the drug Cyclone was created to treat?" he asked.

Dr. Warren nodded. "Exactly."

"Tell me, Dr. Warren," Cole said. "When you fell sick before the police arrived, was it after Diane gave you something to eat or drink?"

Dr. Warren thought for a moment, "Actually, yes, it was. Diane made me a coffee just before the sickness started."

That sealed it for Cole. "We have to find her before she hurts anybody else," he said.

Cole raced toward the elevator, angry with himself for failing to spot the culprit right under his nose. Deborah was in danger, working side by side with someone who was so grief stricken about her baby's disease that she had pushed all her moral standards aside.

How far would Diane go to protect the baby she loved?

The clinical waste unit was a small red plastic bin with *hazardous waste* written on the side. Deborah certainly didn't want to be rummaging around inside, but she was determined to find the missing sample and find out exactly why it was so important to Diane. To her dismay, there was no sign of it and she stood up straight, snapping off the latex gloves she had been wearing and depositing them in the trash.

She walked into the corridor and considered her next move. Then she saw Diane at the end of the corridor, swiping her ID card through security, before leaving the unit. Deborah jogged to the end of the corridor to follow.

Diane walked straight past the elevator and pushed open the door leading to the staircase. Deborah followed at a distance. When Diane exited on the main first floor hallway, they were both absorbed into a throng of people. This hallway was always busy with gurneys, wheelchairs and visitors trying to find their way around, so Deborah felt well shielded in case Diane turned around. She felt disloyal to her friend for being suspicious of her actions, but Diane was holding something back, and Deborah needed to know what it was.

Diane stopped. Deborah positioned herself behind a payphone and peeked out. Diane hovered outside the re-habilitation unit, did a quick check both ways and went inside. Deborah again followed, using her swipe card to gain access.

The rehabilitation unit was warm and Deborah felt her neck becoming moist. The patients in rehab were mostly elderly and required a higher temperature than others parts of the hospital. The nurses for this hushed and sedate unit usually congregated in the station at the end of the corridor, so the hallway was quiet. The individual rooms had windows facing the hall, and all had their blinds raised. All except one. Deborah felt her pulse race with nervous anticipation as she walked toward the room and rested her fingers on the handle.

Opening the door, she saw an elderly man lying in bed with an oxygen mask over his face. He appeared to be unconscious. The urine sample was sitting on the bed-side cabinet with a syringe balanced on top. But where was Diane?

Stepping into the room, Deborah's question was quickly answered as a pinprick stung her neck and a powerful sensation caused her muscles to lose all strength. She sank to the floor like a popped balloon.

She heard the lock of the door click into place and saw Diane's white sneakers step over her prone body.

She was alone with a woman who wanted to hurt her.

TWELVE

Cole rang the buzzer on the pediatric unit's internal door and waited impatiently for someone to answer. Dr. Warren lagged a long way behind, unable to keep up with his frantic pace.

It was Frank Carlisle who opened the door and allowed him inside.

"Where's Diane?" Cole asked, his eyes darting through the corridor. "I think she's our Cyclone suspect."

Frank was stunned into silence for a second or two. "I'm not sure where Diane is," he replied. "But you must be mistaken. Diane would never do this."

Cole had another, more terrifying thought. "Where's Deborah?"

"I have no idea," Frank said. "The police are waiting to interview her. She's vanished from the unit."

The blood flowing through Cole's veins seemed to turn deathly cold. "We need to find her quickly. She may be with Diane."

Frank put his palms in the air. "Calm down, Mr. Strachan," he said slowly. "What is all this about?"

Dr. Warren appeared behind him, breathless and rosy cheeked from the exertion of running. She explained the situation to Frank, stressing that she suspected Diane's baby to be suffering from cystic fibrosis. Frank's face grew darker with each word.

"This gives her a strong motive for wanting to continue testing Cyclone on the children here," Frank said. "We should tell the police immediately."

Cole felt his anxiety heighten as the seconds passed. "What if Deborah has already uncovered the truth?" he said "She could be in serious danger." He began to walk down the corridor, checking in every room.

"She's not here," Frank repeated. "I already looked all over."

"Well, look again," Cole said with a raised voice, causing passing medical staff to turn and stare.

"I'll put out an announcement and organize a search party," Frank said. "Let's go speak to the police."

Cole knew that they were in the so-called golden hour—that vital short space of time during which a missing person was usually found alive. Once the golden hour passed, the chance of finding a person alive dropped drastically.

"That's a good plan," Cole said, feeling every second tick by like a warning chime. "But I'll start my search immediately."

"You're not authorized to enter any rooms other than the public ones," Frank replied. "You'll have to wait for official help."

"It's okay, Frank," Dr. Warren said. "I'll go with him." She turned to Cole. "Where do you want to start?"

He tried to put himself in Deborah's shoes. Where would she be likely to go in her pursuit of the truth?

"Show me where you store and dispose of medicines, and then we'll work through the patient rooms," he said. "I want to leave no stone unturned."

* * *

Deborah tried to pull herself up to stand but her muscles simply refused to work normally. She managed to grab the door handle for support and rise to her knees, but quickly slumped to the floor again, half leaning against the door. Although her body was as weak as a kitten's, her mind was still sharp and alert.

"What did you give me?" she asked, slurring her words.

Diane turned and looked at her. "Ketamine," she said in a matter-of-fact way. "It's a strong dose, so don't try to fight it." She placed the empty syringe on the bedside cabinet. "I knew you'd gotten suspicious and might try to follow me, so I came prepared."

Deborah swallowed away a buildup of saliva in her mouth, desperately willing her useless limbs to move. But she knew that ketamine was a powerful sedative, often administered to patients undergoing painful treatment, causing temporary paralysis of the muscles.

She lifted her head. It was the only part of her body that she could control. "What are you doing, Diane?" she asked, speaking slowly so she could formulate the words correctly. Her lips felt as if they belonged to somebody else.

Diane held up another syringe that she had filled with the liquid from the specimen jar. Deborah watched in amazement, suddenly aware of how Diane had managed to smuggle Cyclone into the unit and prevent it being discovered. Cyclone's color and consistency had provided Diane with the perfect hiding place, as nobody would question a urine sample being in a hospital.

"I don't expect you to understand," Diane said with a detachment that struck fear into Deborah. "And I don't expect you to care. I'm simply doing what I need to do to save my baby." A sob broke through her emotionless face, and she covered her mouth with a hand to stifle her cry. "My son has cystic fibrosis," she said through her fingers.

Deborah felt a surge of conflicted emotions— sympathy for her friend and bitter resentment for the young lives Diane had put in jeopardy by testing this illegal drug.

"It's useless, Diane," Deborah slurred. "Cyclone doesn't work."

Diane became more animated at this suggestion. "But it *could* work," she said. "I got a guy in the lab to help tweak the formula and alter the dose." She expelled the air from the syringe. "I think I have it just about right, but I need to test it one last time."

"You bribed the lab guy?" Deborah said, remembering how much money had changed hands.

"I remortgaged my house," Diane replied. "I've spent every penny I have to cure my baby. When I found out my unborn son had cystic fibrosis five months ago, the Cyclone trial was my only hope. After the trial failed, I was devastated. I couldn't let all that research go to waste. I knew we had an opening here for a pediatric doctor, and I persuaded Frank to offer the job to a brilliant doctor who had just vacated his position at Shoreline Medical Center." She laughed scornfully. "I knew Frank couldn't resist recruiting a doctor with the credentials of Dr. Cortas."

"You stole the Cyclone from Dr. Cortas's home." Deborah's tongue was lolling inside her mouth. "It was you."

Diane raised her hands in the air, still holding the syringe. "That was like a gift," she said. "I tried to get Dr. Cortas to talk about his past research, but I hit a brick wall time after time. It became clear that he was too cowardly to continue his cystic fibrosis research, so I knew I'd have to do it on my own. So I copied his door key and went looking for the Cyclone paperwork in his home." Her eyes widened in a theatrical gesture. "Imagine how I felt when I found actual vials of Cyclone." She held out her palms. "To hold the potential cure for my son's disease in my own hands was incredible."

Deborah concentrated on breathing deeply to stop herself from panicking. She couldn't imagine Diane allowing her to live. Not now that she knew everything.

"F-f…" Deborah moistened her lips. "Flowers."

Diane wound a band tightly around the elderly man's arm. "I read about Harold Flowers in the *Chicago Tribune* while following the Cyclone story, and I tracked him down."

"You told him lies about me," Deborah slurred. "I thought we were friends."

Diane stopped what she was doing and focused on Deborah. "Please believe me when I say that I had no choice but to do what I did. When you started pushing for an investigation into the kidney failures in Pediatrics, I knew I'd have to find a way to stop you. I thought Harold Flowers would just scare you off. I never thought he'd be so violent." She looked toward the ceiling. "It's probably a good thing that he's dead."

Deborah could see Diane tapping the arm of the patient, trying to find a vein. "No," she said, attempting to raise her voice. "You almost killed a child already. No more, Diane. No more."

The mention of the children in Pediatrics caused Diane's mask to slip a little further. "I'm sorry about the children I made sick," she said. "I really am. That's why I chose an old man for my next experiment." She looked down at the patient in the bed, his papery-thin skin looking so delicate that it might tear. "He's already lived his life."

Deborah rallied her strength. "That doesn't give you the right to take it away."

Diane grew angry. "What about the rights of my baby?" she demanded through gritted teeth. "Why should he suffer?"

Deborah desperately wished Cole were there. He could reach out to Diane. He could sympathize and connect with her, because he'd been through a similar level of pain. Yet he retained a sense of goodness. Despite all the suffering he had endured, Cole still trusted in God and didn't wallow in misery. He was a strong and honorable man, and she loved him more than ever before.

Deborah tried hard to concentrate on keeping her eyes open as Diane continued to rant about the unfairness of her situation. Why had she insisted on forcing Cole to stay away? If she had allowed him to come back as he'd wanted to, there would be some hope for her. If only she hadn't been so stubborn.

The consequences of that bad decision could be fatal.

Cole felt a sense of despondency settle somewhere deep in his belly. A thorough search of the pediatric unit had yielded nothing—no sign of Deborah and no sign of Diane. He was convinced they would be together. And his gut feeling told him Deborah was in trouble.

Frank came running from the end of the corridor, weaving between the police officers.

"Mr. Strachan," Frank said breathlessly. "I've asked the security department to check the security footage from the areas surrounding the pediatric unit, but it'll take a little while for them to review them all."

Cole could almost hear the seconds of the golden hour ticking by. "We don't have time," he muttered, pacing. "There must be another way." He watched a nurse walk past and her ID badge caught a beam from the overhead light, glinting in his direction. "Of course," he exclaimed, angry with himself for not realizing sooner. "My team installed a new swipe card reader in every department. The entire hospital is now connected to a database. Wherever Deborah is, her ID card will tell us."

He began to run to the small room with the central computer. Frank followed closely at his heels, huffing and puffing loudly with the effort. The small office was dark and cool. Cole flicked on the screen and a white glow was cast over his face. He knew exactly where he needed to go—straight to the hospital security database, where all ID swipes would be logged.

"Come on, come on," he said half under his breath, willing the computer to go faster.

At last the password screen popped up and he stepped back to allow Frank to enter the information. Within seconds he could see hundreds of different data entries tracking every staff member. It was a jumble of letters and numbers that changed by the second. He typed in Deborah's name and waited for her data to be found. When the information came up on screen, he wasted no time. He turned and ran from the room.

"She's in the rehabilitation unit on the first floor," he shouted behind him. "Frank, I need you to show me where it is."

"Wait… Mr.…Strachan," Frank called, struggling to catch his breath. "Let's allow the police to do their job."

He ignored the plea and exited the pediatric unit. He decided not to wait for the elevator but instead took the stairs two at a time until he reached the busy first floor hallway. He looked both ways and stopped an orderly.

"Which way is the rehab unit?" he asked.

The orderly pointed, and Cole set off running again, aware that Frank was behind him leading two police officers to the location. As he ran, Cole called out to medical staff ahead of him, asking for directions. When he saw the sign come into view, he picked up his pace, only to remember that he couldn't open the door without an ID card.

He stopped a nurse outside the door. "I need to get into this unit," he said. "The woman I love may be in danger inside. Can you please let me in?"

A look of surprise flashed over the nurse's face, quickly replaced by one of suspicion. Then she noticed Frank Carlisle running toward them, his suit jacket flapping open and tie trailing in the air behind him. Her eyes widened in confusion.

"It's okay, Nurse," Frank called. "You can let him in."

Cole darted through the door and along the corridor, quickly spotting the only room where the blinds were lowered, preventing anyone from prying inside. He turned the handle of the door. It was locked. He pulled back his shoulder to force the door, only to be drawn back by a police officer.

"We'll handle this, sir," the officer said, then knocked loudly on the door. "This is the police. Open up."

Cole placed his head in his hands. Now they had lost the element of surprise.

There was no reply.

The officer knocked again and repeated his request. Cole's patience was at breaking point. "We're wasting time."

"Stand back, sir," the officer said, pulling out his gun.

Then, with one swift kick, the door burst open to reveal Diane holding a limp and pale figure in her arms on the floor. The blond curls obscured her face, but it was unmistakably Deborah.

Diane glared in their direction. "If you take one more step, she dies." At that moment, Cole noticed the syringe Diane was holding in her hands. It was full of a bright blue liquid, and the tip was firmly placed in Deborah's neck.

"Pull back," he said to the officers. "Lower your weapons."

The two officers lowered their guns slowly and took a step back, uncertain of the contents of the syringe but not willing to take a chance. One wrong move could spell disaster.

"It's okay, Diane," Cole said gently, realizing just how volatile she was at this moment. Her eyes were wide and wild, her skin devoid of color and her lips pinched into an expression of determination. "We don't want to hurt you," he said. "We know you're just trying to protect your baby."

Her wide eyes suddenly narrowed. "What do you know about my baby?"

"Dr. Warren noticed something on your ultrasound," he said, taking small, barely noticeable steps toward the door. "Your baby has cystic fibrosis, right?" Diane's eyes filled with tears. "And you were the one injecting Cyclone into the patients, hoping to continue Dr. Cortas's failed research," he continued, taking more tiny steps toward her. Before she had noticed, he was in the room.

"Stop right there!" Diane shouted, suddenly seeing how far Cole had encroached into her space. "I won't let you stop this last experiment." She looked at the man on the bed. "I need to wait and see if this dose of Cyclone works better than the others. It's my last attempt."

Cole stopped in his tracks. "Diane," he said, bending down to be on her level. "I just want to talk to you. You have my word that I won't hurt you or your baby." He glanced at the man on the bed, praying that the drug Diane had injected wouldn't overcome his frail body.

Diane considered Cole's offer with a hard expression, weighing his words. She looked behind him to the two officers and Frank Carlisle standing in the corridor.

"Shut the door," she said. "And we'll talk. But just you."

Cole turned and closed the door gently, clicking it into place, ignoring the officers, who shook their heads, clearly not happy to be shut out. He then turned back to Diane and squatted to the floor, putting one knee on the tiles and resting his forearm on the other. Deborah stirred and a sound came from her mouth. Cole felt a fluttering in his chest. She was okay. Obviously drugged, but okay.

"I lost a child," he said, deciding to come right out with it. "A son named Elliot. He died when he was three months old. I would've done almost anything to save him."

Diane listened intently, her fingers trembling on the syringe in Deborah's neck. "Would you have done the same as me?"

Cole shook his head. "No."

Diane gave a little snort. "Then you're a terrible father."

There had been many times when Cole had thought this exact thing. But he knew better now. "Being a good parent isn't about your ability to protect your child from harm," he said. "It's about your ability to love them."

"I'd sooner love a living child than a dead one," Diane replied. "You can't truly love a dead child."

"Oh, you can," Cole said with deep emotion. "I do." Deborah began to stir again and he resisted the urge to reach out and touch her, to run his fingers along her face. She needed him to be strong and to defuse the danger in the room.

"Do you think you have a right to take a life in order to save your child?" he asked. "Do you think that's fair?"

Diane stared at him with resentment. "Nothing is fair," she said. "Is it fair that Deborah ends up here with a syringe of thallium in her neck?"

Cole let out a breath and rubbed a hand over his face. Thallium was a common chemical previously used in rat poison, now banned in most states, but still easily purchased online. It could kill Deborah in a large enough dose.

"She doesn't deserve that," he said. "Deborah is a good person who cares deeply about you." He tried to control the shakiness of his voice. "And I love her very much."

Diane's face softened. "I don't want to hurt her," she said, looking up at the old man on the bed. "I just want to be left alone a few minutes while the Cyclone takes effect on this patient. I can't take a blood sample for cell analysis for another hour at least. I think I might've gotten the formula right this time."

Cole heard footsteps outside the door. More officers had arrived. He imagined them bursting into the room, spooking Diane. He thought of her finger pushing down on the syringe, sending the poison coursing through Deborah's veins.

"Hold off," he called out behind him. "It's not yet safe."

The movement stopped, and he breathed a sigh of relief.

Cole pointed to Diane's belly. "The kingdom of heaven belongs to children like ours," he said. "Somebody reminded me of that recently."

"Children like ours?" Diane questioned.

"Children who are weak in body but pure in heart and spirit," he replied. "Your baby will be loved by many, especially God. And his riches will be stored up in heaven."

Cole could see tears running down Diane's face. The syringe began to droop.

"It's not too late to save this man," Cole continued, pointing to the patient on the bed. "It's not too late to do the right thing."

Deborah gave a low moan, clearly trying to communicate. Diane shifted her position and Deborah's head lolled back. Cole's stomach lurched as the syringe moved in her neck, but Diane managed to keep it steady.

Deborah mumbled some words, mostly incomprehensible, but Cole thought he heard the word *forgiveness*.

"It's not too late to ask for forgiveness," he said. A small smile passed over Deborah's lips.

Diane moved her fingers from the syringe and rested them over her belly. "I just wanted to do the best for my boy," she sobbed. "I wanted to fight for him."

Cole thought of the precious bond that existed between a parent and child. It was an amazing, unshakable connection that reflected God's enduring love for His children. And Cole wanted to feel it again. Without question.

"There are plenty of ways to fight for someone, Diane," Cole said soothingly. "But unless you fight with a pure heart, you'll never achieve anything good." He locked eyes with Deborah. "When I have more children, I'll never give up on them while they live and never stop loving them if they pass. You can't control how your kids turn out, but you can do your best to be a good example."

Cole felt the tension in the room lifting. He sensed that Diane was truly listening to him.

"I thought I could make sure my son was a strong, capable man," Diane said quietly, moving her hand from her belly and back to the syringe. "Instead of someone who needs nursing his whole life."

"Some of the strongest men I know are missing limbs or in wheelchairs and need help on a daily basis," Cole said, thinking of the many veterans he had had the privilege of serving with. He rested his index finger on his temple. "True strength comes from in here."

Diane's shoulders sagged as if the weight of the world were pressing down on them. "I'll go to jail, I guess," she said. "After everything I've done."

Cole didn't want to distress Diane just when he could see light at the end of the tunnel, but neither did he want to lie to her. "That's pretty likely," he replied. "But you haven't caused anyone to die yet, and I don't want the death of this elderly man to be on your conscience. If you take responsibility for your actions, you can accept the punishment and ask for forgiveness." He reached out his hand. "It really is that simple."

She didn't take his hand, and his fingers hung limply in the air.

"Diane," he said with a slightly harder edge to his voice as he noticed her index finger twitching on the end of the syringe. "If you allow any of that poison to enter Deborah's bloodstream, you'll be destroying two people's lives, not just one."

Diane looked at him in confusion for a couple of

seconds before she realized what he was saying. "You really love her, huh?" she asked.

He smiled, still holding his hand toward Diane, encouraging her to take it. "Yes, I really love her. And I'd like to finally get around to marrying her and having a family." He made his smile even broader. "And maybe a dog that chases sticks in the yard."

Throughout the time he spoke, he saw Deborah's eyes blink slowly and remain on him constantly. He didn't know how alert her drugged mind was, or if any of his words were sinking into her brain.

"She really loves you, too," Diane said with a nod. "She tried to hide it, but I could tell." She hung her head. "I hated lying to her all this time, but I couldn't see another way."

"There *is* another way," Cole said firmly. "There's always another way."

Diane gave a sigh that seemed to come from a hollow place deep inside, and finally she pulled the syringe out of Deborah's neck, dropped it to the floor and reached over to take Cole's hand. He squeezed it tightly. Her fingers were icy cold and limp, and she tried to return his tight grip, undoubtedly knowing that she didn't deserve his kindness and welcoming it gratefully.

Then Cole drew back his hand, rose to his feet and picked up Deborah in his arms. He struggled to hold her body close as her slack limbs escaped his grasp. She clearly had no muscle control. Yet she could move her head and positioned it in the groove where his shoulder met his neck. The smell and touch of her hair filled him with happiness and relief.

Cole carried her to the door and hooked a finger over the handle. He briefly turned back to Diane. She was sitting on the floor, hands spread over her bump, staring into thin air.

"Keep strong for your baby," he said. "Love him for who he is and he'll love you back always."

Cole then dragged down the handle of the door and swung it open. A sea of police officers stood behind the door, guns raised in anticipation.

Cole jerked his head behind him. "The old man needs medical treatment right away. He's been injected with Cyclone. Diane is on the floor next to the bed, but she won't resist arrest. She's a broken woman."

Frank's head popped up behind the line of officers. "Oh, my!" he said, rushing forward. "What happened to Deborah? Is she okay?"

"She's been drugged, but I think she's fine," he replied. "Let's get her to Dr. Warren." He pushed his way along the corridor as he heard an officer reading Diane her rights.

Frank held open the door of the unit and Cole strode out into the main corridor, holding Deborah tightly against his chest. He could feel her breathing steadily as if she were sleeping. She was mumbling, trying to speak, but the powerful drug had robbed her of the use of her tongue, and her sounds were too slurred to understand.

"Shh," he said into her ear. "Let's get you checked out before you try to speak. Whatever you want to say can wait."

She made a short, sharp noise of frustration, letting him know that she clearly didn't agree. Whatever she wanted to say was important, and he saw urgency in her eyes.

His spirit lifted as he wondered whether maybe she was thinking the same thing as he was. Maybe they had at last overcome the final hurdle.

* * *

Deborah felt a tingling sensation in her toes and wiggled them. Cole stood at the end of the bed, hands on the rail, watching her intently. Under the fluorescent light his eyes seemed to be an unreal shade of green, as though a child had colored them with a bright crayon. His expression was difficult to read—he was neither smiling nor sad. He simply looked at her with an unwavering gaze while Dr. Warren checked her over thoroughly.

"Your vital signs are all perfectly normal, and you have no injuries," Dr. Warren said with a smile. "It'll take another hour or so for the ketamine to fully wear off, but I'm pleased to say you're in good health."

"Where's Diane?"

"She's been arrested," Cole said. "The police have taken her to the station for questioning, but she's being well looked after. The baby's fine."

"And the elderly man?" she asked.

"He's doing okay, too," Cole replied. "He's still unconscious, but recovering."

Deborah pulled herself up to a seated position. "I heard what you said to Diane about her baby. I thought it was beautiful."

Cole looked suddenly awkward. "Did you hear the other things I said?"

Dr. Warren took her cue to leave. "I'll just run these blood samples down to the lab," she said, heading for the door. "I'll be back later."

As soon as the door was closed, Deborah spoke. "Yes, I heard what you said. I heard all of it. I couldn't speak, but my mind was still sharp."

Cole swallowed and rubbed his hands together. She

recognized these gestures as those he always made when he was nervous. It made her laugh.

"What's so funny?" he asked.

"You," she said. "You still do all the same things you did when you were eighteen."

"Well, one thing's for sure," he said, walking around the bed and taking her hand in his. "I still love you as much as I did when I was eighteen." He stopped for a moment. "No, that might not be true. I think I love you *more* than I did at eighteen."

Deborah opened her mouth to speak but Cole brought a finger to her lips.

"Let me finish," he said. "There's more I need to say."

She gave a small nod and Cole cupped her hands in his.

He took a deep breath. "Speaking to Diane gave me a new perspective on things. As I was talking to her about the love a parent feels for their child, I realized how sacred it is. God doesn't want me to be a lonely old man. He doesn't want me to live a life in fear, too afraid to take risks in case I get hurt. I'm pretty sure God wants me to be surrounded by a loving family who makes me feel like the happiest man on earth." He laughed. "Oh, I almost forgot to include a dog." He slapped a palm to his head playfully. "I always forget about the dog."

"What kind of dog?" she asked, playing along.

He grinned. "Not a big slobbering one, that's for sure." The smile left his face. "I wish I'd been able to see things this clearly a few days ago. It would've saved us both a lot of heartache."

"I think you experienced your epiphany right at the perfect time," Deborah said. "It made your words more powerful, like you were healing your own hurt at the same time as Diane's." She squeezed his fingers. "You saved me by just using your voice, and that makes you an incredibly special person."

"Special enough for you to share the rest of your life with?"

"Yes."

"Special enough to be your husband and the father of your children?"

She let out a little squeal, too overwhelmed to keep it inside. "Absolutely."

"In that case," Cole said and took a step back and dropped to a bended knee. "Deborah Lewis, will you grant me my greatest wish and be my wife?" He held out his empty hands. "I don't have a ring yet." His expression changed as an idea clearly pinged in his head, and he teased the heavy gold ring from his pinkie finger and held it up. "We can use my navy SEAL ring until you choose your own."

Deborah shifted herself to the edge of the bed and swung her legs over the side. Her limbs were still a little loose and she almost tipped, but Cole jumped forward and steadied her. Then he slipped the ring onto the third finger of her left hand. It was chunky gold with a bold black insignia, way too big for her slender finger.

"It fits perfectly," she said, holding her fingers aloft. "I love it." She brought her eyes back to Cole, who stood in front of her beaming like a man whose future was full of blessings. "And I love you, Cole."

Her face broke into an uncontrollable smile. She had never imagined those words would be easy for her to say again, but they sounded natural and effortless on her tongue. So she said them again.

"I love you, Cole."

He pressed his lips on hers and she allowed herself to float away on a blissful cloud.

EPILOGUE

Cole walked into the church community center with a surge of excitement. The balloons and banners that decked out the foyer showed how hard Deborah had worked to organize this very special party.

He stopped to look at the notice that had been hung above the door: Congratulations on Your Engagement, Deborah and Cole. He smiled with pride. To see his name next to hers brought him a pleasure like no other.

A flurry of activity overtook him as people with plates of food and bottles of soda filled the foyer.

One of the women looked at him in surprise. It was Lori, Deborah's best friend from high school. "Cole," she said. "You're early." She checked her watch. "Really early."

"Yeah, I know," he said. "But I just couldn't stay away." He shrugged his shoulders. "I'm as excited as a kid at Christmas."

"Well, we have a lot of preparation to do," she said. "Why don't you go grab a coffee or something and give us a while to get everything ready."

"Sure," he said, feeling slight disappointment settle. "I'll get out of your hair."

Lori put down her plate of cakes and stepped outside

for a few seconds. She came back inside with a tall, skinny man by her side.

"My husband is also looking for a way to get out of our hair," she said with a knowing smile. "And by my reckoning, you two are way overdue for a reunion."

Cole extended his hand to his old friend Josh Fenton. "Hi, Josh," he said nervously. "I've been meaning to give you a call."

Josh ignored Cole's hand and enveloped him in a hug. "We've got a lot of catching up to do," he said. "Wanna get out of here for a while? There's a coffeehouse right across the street."

Cole slapped him on the back. "Sounds great. I think there might be a story about a mouse I'd like to talk about."

Josh threw back his head and laughed. "Yeah, I owe you big-time for taking the rap there. The coffee's on me, okay?"

Deborah appeared by Cole's side and linked her arm through his. "I don't need to ask what you two are talking about, right?"

Cole kissed her on the top of her head. "You look beautiful," he said. And he truly meant it. Wearing a tailored dress in a bright shade of red, she stood out for all the right reasons.

"Thank you," she said. "Now you two boys run along and play."

Cole and Josh headed for the door. To be welcomed back into the community so warmly made Cole's heart surge with love—love not just for Deborah but for all the old friends who had given him a second chance.

As he walked out into the cool, clear winter sunshine, Cole glanced back at Deborah to see her watching him leave. The happiness on her face was evident, and she winked at him, flashing her white teeth in a beautiful smile.

He called out behind him. "Love you. See you in an hour."

Cole inhaled a deep breath of pure Harborcreek air into his lungs. God had led him from the darkness into the light. He was back where he belonged. And he was whole again.

* * * * *

Dear Reader,

There are a great many people who inspired me to create the strong and resilient characters of Deborah and Cole, and I admire them all.

The human spirit has a remarkable ability to heal itself from even the most devastating emotional injuries. The loss of a loved one, particularly a child, is a pain too big for words, as Cole found out after the death of his baby son. His reaction to the tragedy was to shut himself off from further heartache and reject the idea of family life. But he was forgetting that there is no mountain God cannot move and no wound too deep for His hands to reach.

With gentle guidance from both Deborah and Dillon, Cole was able to accept his loss and use his past pain to teach Diane how to face her uncertain future with grace and humility. He learned that a tragedy is not the end—it is simply a bend in the road. It is often difficult to keep moving forward when you cannot see around the corner, but faith will carry you through the darkness.

Thank you for sharing in Cole and Deborah's story. I hope you will join me for Dillon's story, the third in my Navy SEAL Defenders series.

Blessings,
Elisabeth

REQUEST YOUR FREE BOOKS!

2 FREE RIVETING INSPIRATIONAL NOVELS PLUS 2 FREE MYSTERY GIFTS

Love Inspired
SUSPENSE
RIVETING INSPIRATIONAL ROMANCE

YES! Please send me 2 FREE Love Inspired® Suspense novels and my 2 FREE mystery gifts (gifts are worth about $10). After receiving them, if I don't wish to receive any more books, I can return the shipping statement marked "cancel." If I don't cancel, I will receive 4 brand-new novels every month and be billed just $4.99 per book in the U.S. or $5.49 per book in Canada. That's a savings of at least 17% off the cover price. It's quite a bargain! Shipping and handling is just 50¢ per book in the U.S. and 75¢ per book in Canada.* I understand that accepting the 2 free books and gifts places me under no obligation to buy anything. I can always return a shipment and cancel at any time. Even if I never buy another book, the two free books and gifts are mine to keep forever.

123/323 IDN GH5Z

Name _____ (PLEASE PRINT)

Address _____ Apt. #

City _____ State/Prov. _____ Zip/Postal Code

Signature (if under 18, a parent or guardian must sign)

Mail to the **Reader Service:**
IN U.S.A.: P.O. Box 1867, Buffalo, NY 14240-1867
IN CANADA: P.O. Box 609, Fort Erie, Ontario L2A 5X3

Are you a current subscriber to Love Inspired® Suspense books and want to receive the larger-print edition? Call 1-800-873-8635 or visit www.ReaderService.com.

* Terms and prices subject to change without notice. Prices do not include applicable taxes. Sales tax applicable in N.Y. Canadian residents will be charged applicable taxes. Offer not valid in Quebec. This offer is limited to one order per household. Not valid for current subscribers to Love Inspired Suspense books. All orders subject to credit approval. Credit or debit balances in a customer's account(s) may be offset by any other outstanding balance owed by or to the customer. Please allow 4 to 6 weeks for delivery. Offer available while quantities last.

Your Privacy—The Reader Service is committed to protecting your privacy. Our Privacy Policy is available online at www.ReaderService.com or upon request from the Reader Service.
We make a portion of our mailing list available to reputable third parties that offer products we believe may interest you. If you prefer that we not exchange your name with third parties, or if you wish to clarify or modify your communication preferences, please visit us at www.ReaderService.com/consumerchoice or write to us at Reader Service Preference Service, P.O. Box 9062, Buffalo, NY 14240-9062. Include your complete name and address.

LIS15

SPECIAL EXCERPT FROM

Love Inspired.
SUSPENSE

*Inheriting her estranged father's house near
Amish country puts this speechwriter in grave danger.*

*Read on for a sneak preview of
PLAIN DANGER by* Debby Giusti.

Bailey's plaintive howl snapped Carrie York awake with a start. The Irish setter had whined at the door earlier. After letting him out, she must have fallen back to sleep.

Raking her hand through her hair, Carrie rose from the bed and peered out the window into the night. Streams of moonlight cascaded over the field behind her father's house and draped the freestanding kitchen house, barn and chicken coop in shadows. In the distance, she spotted the dog, seemingly agitated as he sniffed at something hidden in the tall grass.

"Hush," she moaned as his wail continued. The neighbors on each side of her father's property—one Amish, the other a military guy from nearby Fort Rickman—wouldn't appreciate having their slumber disturbed by a rambunctious pup who was too inquisitive for his own good.

Still groggy with sleep, she pulled on her clothes, stumbled into the kitchen and flicked on the overhead light. Her coat hung on a hook in the anteroom. Slipping it on, she opened the back door and stepped into the cold night.

"Bailey, come here, boy."

Again the dog's cry cut through the night.

The dog sniffed at something that lay at his feet. A dead animal perhaps? Maybe a deer?

"Bailey, come."

The dog glanced at her, then turned back to the downed prey.

A stiff breeze blew across the field. She shivered and wrapped the coat tightly around her neck, feeling vulnerable and exposed, as if someone were watching… and waiting.

Letting out a deep breath to ease her anxiety, she slapped her leg and called to the dog. "Come, boy. We need to go inside."

Reluctantly, Bailey trotted back to where she stood.

"Good dog." She patted his head and scratched under his neck. Feeling his wet fur, she raised her hand and stared at the tacky substance that darkened her fingers.

She gasped. Even with the lack of adequate light, the stain looked like blood.

"Are you hurt?"

The dog barked twice.

Bending down, she wiped her hand on the dew-damp grass, then stepped closer to inspect the carcass of the fallen animal.

Holding her breath to ward off the cloying odor, she stared down at the pile of fabric.

Her heart pounded in her chest. A deafening roar sounded in her ears. She whimpered, wanting to run. Instead she held her gaze.

Not a deer.

But a man.

Don't miss PLAIN DANGER by Debby Giusti,
available February 2016 wherever
Love Inspired® Suspense books and ebooks are sold.

*As a young woman seeks a better life for herself
and her son in Amish country, will she find happiness
and love with an Amish carpenter?*

*Read on for a sneak preview of
A HUSBAND FOR MARI,
the second book in the new series
THE AMISH MATCHMAKER.*

"That's James," Sara the matchmaker explained in English. "He's the one charging me an outrageous amount for the addition to my house."

"You want craftsmanship, you have to pay for it," James answered confidently. He strode into the kitchen, opened a cupboard, removed a coffee mug and poured himself a cup. "We're the best, and you wouldn't be satisfied with anyone else."

He glanced at Mari. "This must be your new houseguest. Mari, is it?"

"*Ya*, this is my friend Mari." Sara introduced her. "She and her son, Zachary, will be here with me for a while, so I expect you to make her feel welcome."

"Pleased to meet you, Mari," James said. The foreman's voice was pleasant, his penetrating eyes strikingly memorable. Mari felt a strange ripple of exhilaration as James's strong face softened into a genuine smile, and he held her gaze for just a fraction of a second longer than was appropriate.

Warmth suffused her throat as Mari offered a stiff nod and a hasty "Good morning," before turning her attention to her unfinished breakfast. Mari didn't want anyone to get the idea that she'd come to Seven Poplars so Sara could find her a husband. That was the last thing on her mind.

"Going to be working for Gideon and Addy, I hear," James remarked as he added milk to his coffee from a small pitcher on the table.

Mari slowly lifted her gaze. James had nice hands. She raised her eyes higher to find that he was still watching her intently, but it wasn't a predatory gaze. James seemed genuinely friendly rather than coming on to her, as if he was interested in what she had to say. "I hope so." She suddenly felt shy, and she had no idea why. "I don't know a thing about butcher shops."

"You'll pick it up quick." James took a sip of his coffee. "And Gideon is a great guy. He'll make it fun. Don't you think so, Sara?"

Sara looked from James to Mari and then back at James. "I agree." She smiled and took a sip of her coffee. "I think Mari's a fine candidate for all sorts of things."

Don't miss
A HUSBAND FOR MARI
by Emma Miller,
available February 2016 wherever
Love Inspired® books and ebooks are sold.